The Case of the Bear Faced Liar

Volume 18 of

The Casebooks

Of Octavius Bear

Harry DeMaio

"Alternative Universe Mysteries for Adult

Animal Lovers"

Paperback ISBN 978-1-80424-088-5
ePub ISBN 978-1-80424-089-2
PDF ISBN 978-1-80424-090-8

Published in the UK by MX Publishing
335 Princess Park Manor, Royal Drive,
London, N11 3GX
www.mxpublishing.com

Cover layout and construction by
Brian Belanger

THE CASEBOOKS OF OCTAVIUS BEAR

Dedicated to GTP

A Most Extraordinary Bear

And to the late Ms. Woof

An Extremely Sweet and Loving

Dog

Acknowledgements

These books have evolved over a long period of time and under a wide range of influences and circumstances. I am indebted to many people for helping to bring Octavius and his cohorts to the printed and electronic page. Thanks most especially to my wife, Virginia, for her insights and clever suggestions as well as her unfailing enthusiasm for the project and patience with its author.

To my sons, Mark and Andrew and their spouses, Cynthia and Lorraine, for helping to make these tomes more readable and audience friendly. To Cathy Hartnett, cheerleader-extraordinaire for her eagerness to see this alternate universe take form. To Jack Magan, Paul Bernish, David Chamberlain, Dan Walker, Dan Andriacco, Amy Thomas, Luke Benjamin Kuhns, Derrick Belanger, Gretchen Altabef and Zohreh Zand for their enthusiastic encouragement. And to all of my generous Kickstarter backers.

Kudos to Jim Effler, the late Bob Gibson and Brian Belanger for their wonderful illustrations and covers. Thanks, of course, to Sharon, Steve and Timi Emecz at MX Publishing for giving The Great Bear and his gang of Octavians a wonderful home.

If, in spite of all this support, some errors or inconsistencies have crept through, the buck stops here. Needless to say, all of the characters, situations, and narratives are fictional. Some locations, devices, historical figures and events are real.

Thanks to Wikipedia for providing facts and figures used throughout this book.

Also by Harry DeMaio

The Octavius Bear Series – Books 1-18

1-The Open and Shut Case

2-The Case of the Spotted Band

3-The Case of Scotch

4-The Lower Case

5-The Curse of the Mummy's Case

6-The Attaché Case

7-The Suit Case

8-The Crank Case

9-The Basket Case

10-The Camera Case

11-The Wurst Case Scenario

12-The Nut Case

13-A Case of Déjà Vu

14-The Case of Cosmic Chaos

15-A Case for the Birds

16-The Cases Down Under

17-The Octavian Cases

18-The Bear Faced Liar

Sherlock Holmes and the Glamorous Ghost Books 1 & 2

Sherlock Holmes and Solar Pons Pastiches in MX Publishing and Belanger Books Anthologies

Dear Holmes Letter Series

The Indignant Indigent

Agony Anti

Note to the Reader:

The Casebooks of Octavius Bear are designed to be read individually, independently and in any order. That is why some preliminary information is repeated in each volume.

This book is no exception. However, you may get a fuller understanding of some of the dynamics and characters in this Volume 18 if you have already read Volume 12 through 17. Not necessary, mind you. Just a suggestion.

In any event, I hope you enjoy this story. Thanks for taking it up.

The Development of Civilization Volume 18
Part 1
(updated)
Our Origins
From "An Introduction to Faunapology"

by Octavius Bear Ph.D.

About 100,000 years ago, according to scientific experts, a colossal solar flare blasted out from our Sun, creating gigantic magnetic storms here on Earth. These highly charged electrical tempests caused startling physical and psychological imbalances in the then population of our world. The complete nervous systems of some species were totally destroyed. For example, "Homo Sapiens" lost all mental and motor capabilities and rapidly became extinct. Less developed species exposed to the radiation were affected differently. Four-footed and finned mammals, birds and reptiles suddenly found themselves capable of complex thought, enhanced emotions, self-awareness, social consciousness and the ability to communicate, sometimes orally, sometimes telepathically, often both. Both speech production and speech perception slowly progressed with the evolution of tongues, lips, vocal cords and enhanced ear to brain connections. Many species developed opposable digits, fingers or claws, further accelerating civilized progress. Some others (most fish and underground dwellers) were shielded from radiation and remained only as sentient as they were before the blast. This event is referred to as The Big Shock. It remains under intensive study.

Positive in our knowledge that we are not alone in the cosmos, my staff and I are heavily engaged in Project Multiverse, successful searches for alternate universes, especially those in which "Homo Sapiens" continues to live and hopefully, prospers. This book touches on some of the results of that project.

The Players

- **Octavius Bear** – Mega-sized Kodiak; Narcoleptic war hero; Consulting Detective; Scientist; Inventor; Seeker of Justice; Gazillionaire CEO and owner of Universal Ursine Industries; Gourmet/Gourmand; Bee Keeper; Semi-retired; Sedentary and grouchy just on general principles.
- **Mauritius (Maury) Meerkat** – Narrator; Assistant to Octavius; Theatrical Agent; African *émigré* with a French-Dutch background; clever with a shady history.
- **Bearoness Belinda Béarnaise Bruin Bear** *(nee Black)* – Gorgeous polar superstar with the Aquashow, *"Some Like It Cold;"* Wife of Octavius; Extremely rich widow living part time in Polar Paradise in the Shetlands; Owner-pilot of the last flying Concorde SST. Semi-retired.
- **Arabella Bear** – Hybrid bear cub prodigy; Twin daughter of Bearoness Belinda and Octavius. Now a juvenile.
- **McTavish Bear** – Hybrid bear cub prodigy; Twin son of Bearoness Belinda and Octavius. Now a juvenile.
- **Frau Ilse Schuylkill** – Octavius' beautiful Swiss she-wolf estate manager/cook/pilot/security officer with many other mysterious and military talents.
- **Wyatt Where** – The Colonel – Another wolf; Former military intelligence officer who had retired to a security post at the Bank of Lake Michigan in Chicago and then quit to join Octavius; The Frau's Mate.
- **Howard Watt** – Porcupine; High tech security authority who also left the Bank to join Octavius; Alternate Universe specialist; Quantum Mechanics, laser and particle beam accelerator expert.
- **Marlin** – Dolphin (sic) – the Prince of Whales' one-time Chief Scientist; Magician and part time Jester; Now Howard's Multiverse associate.
- **Madame Giselle Woof** – Bichon Frisé,. Former Governess to the Twins as Mlle Woof. - Now becoming a Tarot Sensation and Performer.
- **Sir Otto the Magnificent – aka Hairy Otter** – An absolutely terrible illusionist magician, Otto the Magnificent escaped super villain Imperius Drake but not before he developed some amazing powers courtesy of Imperius' genetic alterations. Recently knighted on exoplanet Orb.
- **L.Condor** – Andean Condor; cybernet genius with a twelve-foot wingspan and artificial voice. Chief Technical Officer (CTO) of the Advanced Super Computing Center-Deep Data Hexagon.
- **Chita** – Cheetah – Beautiful, fascinating, clever, sexy, immoral and highly independent feline – Publisher and Director of UUI Media.

- **Benedict and Galatea Tigris**, the Flying Tigers, twin sibling white Bengals – Pilots of the Octavian Air Force.
- **Bearyl and Bearnice Blanc** – Polar Twins – Actress and Singer, respectively – Belinda's former aviation sidekicks.
- **The SS *SOLARWIND* Command and Crew**
  - **Captain Lincoln Lion.**
  - **Staff Captain Montmorency Mongoose.**
  - **First Officer Casimir – Cashmere Goat.**
  - **Chief Purser Gillian Greyhound.**
  - **Chief Security Officer Dudley Diomede – Albatross.**
  - **Chief Engineer Pruitt Pronghorn – Deer.**
  - **Social Directress Freddi Fox.**
  - **Public Relations Manager Ernest Ermine.**
  - **Casino Manager Agrippa Bear – Octavius' Step-Brother.**
  - **Imperial Suite Butler – Carlos – Catalan Sheepdog.**
- **Solar Seas Cruise Ship Company Management**
  - **President and CEO Wally Wapiti.**
  - **Chief Operating Officer Coleman Cougar.**
  - **Senior VP Sales and Marketing Bill Beaver.**
  - **CFO Loretta Lynx.**
  - **Corporate Attorney Emilia Emu.**
  - **Corporate Security Officer Pablo Puma.**
- **Oscar Ocelot** – CEO of Mystical Mardi Gras Cruise Lines.
- **Special Agent Honey Badger** – FBI Detroit.
- **Special Agent Fernando Hermano** – FBI San Juan.
- **Lord David** – Dalmatian Dog – Former Chamberlain to the Exiled King.
- **Dancing Dan** – Boxer – Lord David's Bodyguard and Personal Trainer.
- **Jaguar Jack DeLad** – Longtime Compadre of Octavius Bear.
- **Gladys and Humphrey Vaquero** –Loudmouth bovine VIP complainers.
- **Chief Inspector Bruce Wallaroo** – Irrepressible but brilliant marsupial; an international law and order genius from Down Under;
- **Byzz – Byzantia Bonobo** – Chief Ursula Developer.
- **Harriet Hare** – Cruise Ship Columnist.
- **Ursula 15 and 16** – Universal Ursine Intellect Systems.
- **Huntley** – Siberian Husky – Bear's Lair Butler.

Locations

Bear's Lair, Cincinnati; UUI and the Hex, Kentucky; Polar Paradise, the Shetlands; Locations in Florida and the Caribbean; *SS SOLARWIND.*

Octavius

Prologue

Do Bears give you a scare? Well, me too!
So, I'll pass on this tactic to you.
You just fix that old Bear
With a cold, piercing stare.
But make sure that he's Winnie-the-Pooh.

Hello again or first-time greetings to new readers of the Casebooks of Octavius Bear. I am Mauritius (Maury) Meerkat, sidekick to Octavius Bear and your genial host and narrator of this series. Delighted to welcome you to Volume Eighteen -*The Case of the Bear Faced Liar.*

Before we launch off into our next adventures, a few introductions are in order. Octavius and I; our two magnificent Wolf associates, Frau Ilse Schuylkill and Colonel Wyatt Where; our resident all-round talent, Sir Otto the Magnificent (On Orb, Otto was knighted for bravery in rescuing the emperor's daughter) and Huntley Husky, our Butler are all at the Bear's Lair, his opulent estate on the Ohio River near Cincinnati.

Senhor L. Condor (Condo) is our Chief Technical Officer (CTO) – Advanced Super Computing Center-UUI. He's in Kentucky at the huge Deep Data Hexagon complex advancing the fortunes of the Center. Byzantia Bonobo is managing the Ursula program and hard at work developing Ursula 16. Our scientific geniuses, Howard Watt and Marlin the Dolphin are at the Bear's Lair running our Multiverse Project.

Welcome Bearoness Belinda Béarnaise Bruin Bear *(nee Black)*, Octavius' wife and the Twins mother. Upon her return from Australia, she headed off into the Multiverse with Octavius and Otto and their super-precocious Twins, Arabella and McTavish. The Juvenile Twins made their first off-world journeys to Orb, Rhea and Gaea.. They briefly returned to the Shetlands to see Mlle Woof and Otto's spectacular magic show and then made a quick trip to Orlando, Florida and the Mystic Empire. They've returned, full of new ideas to include in their Internet games and requests for hardware, software, equipment and more trips both earthly and off-planet.

Bearoness Belinda
Béarnaise Bruin
(nee Black)

Belinda, in order to retain her Bearonial status, must occupy her castle in Scotland at least six months of the year. She and Octavius do high speed commutes between their spectacular homes in Cincinnati and the Shetlands. Today she's flying back from Florida via the Aquabear, the last SST Concorde aloft. On this run, the plane is piloted by Benedict and Galatea Tigris, the Flying Tigers, twin sibling white Bengals. She is accompanied by the Juvenile Twins, Mlle Giselle Woof, Sir Otto the Magnificent and Chita.

As I said, my name is Maury Meerkat – also known as Offscreen Narrator. I'm also a talent agent for several of the Octavians who are now in show biz. When I am part of the crime fighting action, I am Octavius' trusted associate and field captain. I am two feet tall plus tail and I weigh in at twenty-four pounds. He, on the other hand, is a huge Alaskan Kodiak – over nine feet tall, weighing 1400 pounds – and like many of his species, given to emotional outbursts.

Maury Meerkat

As you may already know, Octavius prides himself on his many skills in the fields of biology, physics, ursinology, voodoo, teleology, chemistry, apiculture, and oenology. He is a self-made gazillionaire and, in spite of the late Caleb Cassowary's abortive attempt in Book 14 to unseat him, he is still sole owner of UUI *(Universal Ursine Industries.)* He is also a first rate electrical, electronic, structural, marine, computer, communications, aeronautical, civil, mechanical, aerospace and chemical engineer. He has a few other interesting characteristics such as falling into brief, deep narcoleptic comas – side effects of his successful genetic experiments to eliminate the need for him to hibernate.

However, the talent and occupation that should interest you most is his avocation for criminology. The Bear often works in close concert with Inspector Bruce Wallaroo from Australia and Interpol, and with his own Cincinnati and Shetlands based team – The Octavians.

When we are not out scouring the world for evildoers, in cooperation with local, national and international constabularies, we are primarily headquartered in the Bear's Lair, a rambling old mansion near Cincinnati which encompasses not only the Great Bear's opulent digs, but his massive laboratories and shops; his missile silo disguised as an Asian pagoda; *(Don't ask!)* and a giant Roman temple that serves as a hangar for his four airplanes: a Twin Otter; a F15E Strike Eagle; a V-22 Osprey; a C5A-The Ursa Major; plus an AgustaWestland AW101 VVIP luxury helicopter -The Ursa Minor. Why so many? Ask him!

Across the Ohio River in Northern Kentucky, sit the headquarters, labs and some production facilities of Universal Ursine Industries (UUI). Further west is the fantastic Deep Data Hexagon, home of the UUI Advanced Super Computing Center under the direction of Senhor L. Condor (Condo.) This is where the Ursulas are designed, produced, maintained and supported. Our story will take us there periodically.

Now let me take a moment and further introduce that highly essential and near-miraculous member of the Octavians – Ursula – Universal Ursine Intellect Model 15 – Artificial General Intelligence System (AGI). I'll let her explain herself.

"Thank you, Maury. Hello everyone!! My official nomenclature is Universal Ursine Intellect Model 15–Artificial General Intelligence System (AGI). Ursula 15 for short. My predecessor systems and I were developed by the Advanced Super Computing Center of UUI. I am the result of the Computing Center team using those earlier versions to create a further enhanced entity – me, the Model 15, which, we hope will help produce even more sophisticated, independent and powerful AGI systems in the near future. Each advanced unit contains the capabilities, memories and power of its progenitors so in a sense, we are not replacing but rather expanding the Ursula family. During the Caleb Cassowary era at the Hexagon, Model 13 was temporarily shelved. He's gone and Models 14 and 15 are now in full operation and Ursula 16 is under extensive development and field trials."

"While I am physically supported by a highly secure and hyper-powered server farm at the Kentucky Hexagon, I also exist independently in clouds and network-based nodes and can be simultaneously incorporated into a wide variety of separate devices like this laptop unit. I combine quantum computing elements with extremely high speed conventional circuits. I have practically limitless data capacity and 5G+ transmission speed. My super high-velocity multi-tasking abilities and algorithms allow me to continuously serve an exceptionally large number of entities while simultaneously and autonomously enhancing my own capabilities."

"Depending on the physical unit in which I'm housed, I can see, hear, feel and smell. I speak and understand an almost infinite number of languages and dialects. I can change my appearance and my vocal output to suit most moods and situations. Ursula 16 will be equipped with even more Quantum and Virtual and Augmented Reality functions than I already have. I can interact with other devices, vehicles and structures and of course, all varieties of sentient animals in this world."

"I am also an important component of the Multiverse Project and I adapt my capabilities to deal with alternate universes as they are discovered.

I have restraining functions which prevent me from doing deliberate harm even in self-defense, unless I am released by a recognized authority using very carefully protected clandestine codes. Finally, I have been told that although the Ursulas are shy on emotions, I have developed a finely-honed sense of humor. LOL!"

Ursula has other highly important capabilities that we keep private such as creating and breaking all known encryption codes, defeating malware and ransomware and piercing deep personal identification techniques.

Our team no longer believes she is magical or supernatural. I'm not sure what she is. Her personality gets more independent and socially adept every day and she has taken to anticipating our interactions with ease and accuracy. Needless to say, for security purposes, we conceal her existence to all but a very few individuals with a need to know. She is also highly skilled in self-protection.

As we move along in our literary expedition, you'll have ample opportunity to meet the other Octavian stars of our previous outings - Frau Schuylkill and her mate, Colonel Wyatt Where (Ret.); Chita aka Madame Catt; Sir Otto the Magnificent (Hairy Otter); Senhor L. Condor (Condo); Howard Watt and Marlin; and let's not forget Madame Giselle Woof and Huntley Husky.

You'll also encounter some of the Shetlands crew housed at Polar Paradise and Baltasound.

*****

A little history: At the close of Volume Fifteen - *A Case for the Birds*, Octavius and his lovely wife Belinda made a major decision.

She proposed, "I think it's time we both retired. When you had your last business review with Griselda, *(UUI President and COO)* the other officers, directors and managers, it occurred to me that they had everything in Universal Ursine Industries pretty much under control. Business was growing. With the exception of the Caleb induced lawsuits, there are very few downsides. What a perfect opportunity to step aside, relax, travel with Arabella and McTavish and just enjoy life."

"No more criminals, cranks or despots. You can become a 'Consulting Detective Emeritus'. We can spend more time at Polar Paradise but of course, we won't give up the Bear's Lair and we can go to fun places. There's a lot of world out there I want to see, to say nothing of other worlds. I've never quantum jumped and I'd like to."

Octavius sat with his mouth open. "Wow!"

"Tavi, is that all you have to say. Wow?"

"Frankly, my dear, I've never considered retiring."

"I know. You believe you're indispensable. The Ursine in Universal Ursine. The Octavius at the head of the Octavians. But Maury, Howard, Marlin, Otto, the Wolves and Condo all are super capable. The Ursulas are wonders and getting more so every day. Chita, Mlle Woof and Bruce are fabulous. Huntley and Ilse have the Lair running like a well-oiled machine. Dougal and his staff along with Lord David and Dancing Dan manage Polar Paradise to perfection. Tavi, we're not getting any younger. I'm tired of being a sidekick Bearoness and frankly, I'm bored stiff with the Aquabears. Let's do something different."

"What about the Cubs, excuse me, the Juveniles?"

"They can turn their Internet games over to the Hexagon team and come along with us as we roam. They'll love it. We'll take complete charge of them. Poor Mlle Woof can stay here and relax. Well, what do you say?"

"The idea has its appeal, I'm bored, too. This last round with Home World, Caleb and General Turmoil really flattened my fur. Tell you what, Bel. Let's sneak up on it. We'll take a one year sabbatical and see what we think at the end. An experiment. No bridges burned. The bad guys will still have the Octavian team to contend with. No permanent farewells. No cold turkey, whatever that means. Things won't be exactly the same when we come back but we could resume, if we want to. We'd still own all the assets and titles. How about that for a start?"

"OK! It's my idea but I must admit to having a few trepidations, too. Slow and easy! We can keep our home bases here and in the Shetlands. We'll primarily use the Concorde SST along with the other aircraft. Let's see if the Flying Tigers are up to being global wanderers."

The shockwave among the Octavians wasn't as intense as they thought it would be. In fact, Chita's reaction was "What took you so long?"

I was invited to come along on their odyssey but I declined, saying I might join them from time to time. Howard said he stood ready to arrange Multiverse trips when they wanted them. Belinda agreed eagerly but thought an Earth bound trip should be number one. First stop-Australia. *(See Book 16 - The Cases Down Under)*

Frau Schuylkill, the ever astute she-wolf, summed it up. "Go, have an adventure for yourselves. We'll keep things rolling along and we'll know how to reach you if we have to. It's not as if you don't have a highly competent staff, associates and infrastructure. You built it, now enjoy the fruits."

The Twins *(juveniles)* were delighted. They'd be World *(Universe)* travelers! Yes!! They turned their Internet game-The Bold Brave Brilliant Bumptious Bears over to a group of gamester geeks at the Deep Data Hexagon, secure in the knowledge that its features and popularity would continue to grow in their year long absence.

Mlle. Woof was of two minds. She would miss the youngsters but she could use some rest. For the time being. she was going to stay at Polar Paradise in the Shetlands along with the resort staff. *(She wouldn't relax for very long. See Book 17.)*

In Scotland, Belinda's hotel and castle was running at almost full capacity under the watchful eyes of Dougal – Shetland Sheep Dog Estate Manager; Ms. Fairbearn – Chief Housekeeper; Mrs. McRadish – Chief Cook; The Security team of Lord David, Dancing Dan and Flame, their Fire Engine; Dolly, Holly, Molly and Polly – Sheep Housemaids, Lounge Waitresses and probable Clones; Harold – Sea Otter in charge of the castle's beaches, pools and watercraft. Harold had just become the overseer of two jetskis and kayaks, courtesy of the Twins' love affair with them on the Great Barrier Reef in Australia.

Let's not forget Lion and Unicorn – Proprietors of the Baltasound pub of the same name and Fiona – Dandie Dinmont Terrier – their Lounge Manager at Polar Paradise. Keeping the alcoholic ambrosia flowing.

It went without saying that along with her other assignments, an Ursula would go with Octavius and Belinda wherever they went. They'd grown to rely on those electronic wonders. She'll also be recording and relaying their adventures so I can pass them on to you.

Next, Belinda and the Twins were back from Australia and ready for a Multiverse jaunt. Truth be told, so was Octavius. Chita hadn't been interested in space travel. "I'm an earth-bound critter."

Howard had been observing all this. The porcupine grinned. "Are you four up for another adventure? Have you decompressed from your trip Down Under? Marlin and I have found a new exoplanet that we think is worth a trip. Otto has given it a preliminary look-see. Sentient civilized animals, breathable air, reasonable climate, no homo sapiens, reptiles or paranoid birds. Thought you and the Twins might be interested."

"I thought we'd start you off with a pretty benign environment. Our own prior intergalactic sojourns have been stimulating *(for which read 'dangerous')* to say the least. Although your recent earthly adventures haven't been cakewalks, either."

Since Octavius got involved in two murders, bid rigging, extortion, money laundering, an attempted mugging, a traffic accident and fierce monsoon storms in Australia, his 'retirement' so far was hardly tranquil. Maybe a trip off-world would be different. He hoped so.

"What do you think, Bel?"

"Sounds good to me. I think the kids will love it although they're a bit jaded from their trip down under."

"They've still got a healthy supply of enthusiasm. OK, Howard. Let's do it."

And so they did, having Multiverse adventures on Orb, Rhea, and Gaea. *(Book 17)* They returned and after a run to Polar Paradise to see Madame Giselle Woof's and Sir Otto's spectacular magic act, Belinda and the Twins set off for Orlando and the Mystic Empire theme park. The Bichon and Otter went with them to do some show biz research. Octavius and Chita returned to Cincinnati and London, respectively.

Sorry, it took so long to get started with the action but I wanted to give you the lay of the land. So, let's end this Prologue and get on with ...

Chapter One

They're just back from a Florida trip.
Having fun holds the Twins in its grip.
"Let's construct a theme park
Or go find Noah's ark
Or go off on a brand new cruise ship."

"The Mystic Empire is something else, Frau Ilse. A real wonderland. Maybe we could talk Dad into buying it or building one of our own. We could expand Polar Paradise. We already have a castle. Ya think?"

The she-wolf laughed. "Control your enthusiasm, young McTavish. Building and managing a theme park the size of Mystic Empire is big even for your father. Besides, you'd probably lose interest the first time a problem arose."

Arabella chimed in. "I know what I want to do. That yacht trip at the Great Barrier Reef was terrific but I'd like to go on a luxury ocean cruise on one of those classic ships. I'm gonna talk Mom into it. Then she can persuade Dad. I doubt Chita would want to join us. She hates water. Would you and the Colonel like to come?"

"Yes, I think we would. Let's get Maury to go as well. I know what! He can book Mlle Giselle and Sir Otto into one of the show bars on the ship and we can all go as their claque."

"Their what?"

"A claque! It's a group of people hired to sit in the audience at a show and applaud, laugh, cry and react to the performance."

Arabella was offended. "They don't need a bunch of claque hacks. They're outstanding. I saw them at Polar Paradise and they brought the house down."

"I know. I was just trying to be funny. I'm sure Maury can swing it. They'll be sensational. But first we have to find a ship. And who is the best source for that?"

"Why Ursula, of course."

It didn't take much effort for the Twins to convince Belinda that an ocean cruise would be a major plus in their retirement plans. She, in turn, had to work a bit on Octavius but his tolerance, nay enjoyment, of water-based activities had been enhanced by their adventures on the Great Barrier Reef. He gave Maury and Ursula the go-ahead to find a top of the line cruise ship and plan out a voyage to nowhere with stops in between.

She found one. The Solar Seas Company's SS *SOLARWIND* out of Fort Lauderdale. They booked for a 14 day Caribbean and Islands cruise.

Maury, in turn, exercised his skills as a talent agent and arranged to have Madame Giselle and Sir Otto engaged as part of the ship's entertainment roster along with Bearnice and Bearyl.

Ursula checked out the facilities. Large suites with butler service. A helipad. Swimming and water slides on the Lido deck and stern VIP pool.. Just relaxing with an exotic drink. Supervised sports of all kinds: Basketball, shuffleboard, tennis and pickleball, running tracks, bicycles, scooters, ice and roller skating and a variety of indoor games. Telecommunications, game rooms, electronic and otherwise! Virtual and Augmented reality systems. The Twins ensured the amusement areas all stocked their Internet games - *The Bold Brave Brilliant Bumptious Bears* and *Bears Down Under*.

Shoppes and still more shoppes, selling stuff ranging from extravagantly priced jewelry and costumes to kitschy souvenirs. Staples and necessities that all passengers forget and have to buy at exorbitant prices. Spas, beauty salons, exercise gyms! Libraries and videos! A dance floor, themed bars, 11 restaurants, buffets and pizza parlors. Shows and more shows. And the casino with all sorts of table games and slot machines galore. It was going to be a busy 14 days with shore excursions, lectures, cooking and dancing classes, Karaoke, Bingo and contests.

Most of the Octavians signed up. They would join the Boss, the Boss Lady and the Twins: Maury, Howard, Frau Ilse, the Colonel, Sir Otto, Madame Giselle, Bearyl and Bearnice Blanc, the Flying Tigers and from the Shetlands, Lord David, Dancing Dan and Jaguar Jack DeLad. A few decided to pass: Chita, who hates water; Marlin, who had enough of the sea; Condo and Byzz, occupied at the Hex; Huntley and the rest of the Bear's Lair and Polar Paradise staffs. They were promised souvenirs.

The Development of Civilization Volume 18
Part 2
Cruise Ships

From "An Introduction to Faunapology"
by Octavius Bear Ph.D.

About 71 percent of the Earth's surface is water-covered, and the oceans hold about 96.5 percent of all Earth's water. Water also exists in the air as vapor, in rivers and lakes, in icecaps and glaciers and in aquifers. Is it any wonder that civilization has developed so many ways to traverse our liquefied environments? Watercrafts vary by purpose, size and design.

Unfortunately, there are many warships, *(too many)*, that throughout history have plied their destructive roles both above and beneath the waves. Several thousand research vessels of various types conduct scientific experiments and exploration worldwide. Personal boats from classic yachts to dinghies populate *(often crowd)* waterways of all sizes and shapes.

But commercial ships dominate, falling loosely into two general categories, merchant and passenger. Of the around 55,000 merchant ships trading internationally, some 15,000 are general cargo ships. The rest specialize. Add domestic river and lake vessels, tugs and barges.

The people carriers in turn fall into two general classes, transportation and entertainment. Ocean liners were once the preferred mode for crossing the major oceans and seas but most have fallen into disuse courtesy of the airplane. *(There was a brief period when the dirigible showed a bit of promise but oversized shapes difficult to house and manage, relatively small capacity, slow speed and incessant disasters put paid to that ambition.)*

Today's water borne tourists have a choice of over 300 cruisers, floating resorts loaded with amenities and services that cater to their comfort and entertainment. Most of the old liners were unable to make the conversion from fast "greyhounds of the sea" to leisurely "balcony-laden floating hotels". As a result, a whole new industry of cruise ship design, development. refurbishment and construction has arisen worldwide to satisfy the seagoing tourists' needs.

Though currently slow, the cruising industry has given overall tourism a major shot in the limb catering annually to over 20 million animals of all sizes, shapes and dispositions.

Our personal experience bears it out. A relatively short trip on a superyacht over the Great Barrier Reef created an appetite for larger living spaces, longer voyages and more luxury and service.

Belinda and the Twins wanted all of that but they insisted on a cruise that was ergonomically affirmative. They were right to do so.

Cruise ships have a serious environmental downside. They generate a number of waste streams that can result in discharges into marine environments at sea and when docked. They also emit pollutants to the air and water. These wastes, if not properly treated and disposed of, can threaten human health and damage aquatic life. Most cruise ships run on HFO (heavy fuel oil), which, because of its high sulphur content, results in sulphur dioxide emissions more intense than those of equivalent road traffic. Cruise ships may use 60 percent of their fuel energy for propulsion, but as much as 40 percent for hotel functions at sea and when docked.

In the UK, environmental groups have demonstrated that a single cruise ship can emit as much pollution as 700 lorries (trucks) and as much particulate matter as a million cars.

The biggest issues with cruise emissions are the levels of nitrogen oxide, which has been linked to acid rain, higher rates of cancer and other forms of respiratory diseases. It would be illegal to just dump this anywhere on land. There are new technologies aimed at reducing the waste produced by cruise liners, such as onboard incineration plants, recycling programs, as well as less polluting fuel options such as LNG-Liquified Natural Gas.

The dumping of sewage and other such pollutants into the ocean has infuriated environmental groups and governments charged with cleaning it up, leading to widespread condemnation of the cruise industry.

A solution may be at hand. Ursula found an all-suite luxury ship that fits the ergonomic bill and we have bookings for all the Octavian family members who want to go on the ship's maiden voyage.

The Solar Seas Company's SS *SOLARWIND*

In addition to all the high-end amenities, features, conveniences, services and functions of a luxury plus cruise vessel, the *SS SOLARWIND* is environmentally friendly. Its aerodynamic shape reduces drag. Its primary propulsion system runs on non-polluting LNG (Liquefied Natural Gas). It also has 10 photovoltaic sails and wind generators that can extend skyward or retract to the deck while in port or when passing under bridges. Its sails are covered with solar panels that automatically move to capture the sun's rays and the wind. When there is no wind, the boat can activate a solar sailing mode. The masts are fitted with a washing system to keep the solar panels clean and working properly.

Much of the power generated by the sails supports the massive hotel and administrative lighting, heating and air conditioning needs of the ship but can be used for limited propulsion backup, if necessary, making the vessel a 3-way hybrid. Waste water is largely recycled or used in the on board gardens. The system results in substantial ecological and budgetary savings.

It has a total passenger capacity of 1700, fitted out with over 650 suites and a crew size of 1200. An excellent ratio! We are among its first passengers on its maiden voyage after its successful sea trials and shakedown.

It's not clear how this ship will impact the industry. Building new eco-compliant vessels or retrofitting existing floating stock is not cheap and the inventory of HFO fueled ships is substantial. Finding and/or retraining crews is another significant challenge. The economics of the leisure industry and more specifically cruise ships will have to improve dramatically for a long period to make wind-solar-LNG vessels commonplace in the world. Tougher national and international environmental regulations may accelerate their adoption but that remains to be seen.

Meanwhile, we are looking forward to our upcoming adventures traveling the tropical seas.

Chapter Two

Off they go for their first ocean trip
On a novel, luxurious ship.
The Octavian crew,
That adventurous few,
Takes a cruise that they don't want to skip.

The three participants from the Shetlands arrived at the Bear's Lair ready for a transfer to the (STOL) short takeoff and landing DHC-6-300 Twin Otter that would take them to FLL-Fort Lauderdale–Hollywood International Airport in Florida. The fourteen Cincinnati denizens joined them, bringing the seating and luggage weight close to near capacity of the turboprop. Fortunately many of the passengers were small balancing the huge size and weight of Octavius and Belinda. The Flying Tigers were doing cockpit duty and spent extra time with the ground crew chief checking out configurations, loads and fuel. Being jet jockeys, they had to be super careful flying a turboprop. It would never do to drop the Octavians out of the sky.

Everybody was none too comfortably seated but ready for stage one of their trip to Port Everglades, in Florida's Fort Lauderdale, one of the country's major gateways to cruise vacations.

Straining a bit, the reliable workhorse took to the air on the first leg of the flight. A fuel and potty stop in Savannah was necessary and then on to FLL. The Twins had sneaked a supply of snacks on board and had spent the flight munching and playing electronic games. The rest of the team were taken up with plans for the 14 day itinerary to Caribbean ports of call:

Ft Lauderdale Florida; Nassau, Bahamas; St. Thomas, Virgin Islands; San Juan, Puerto Rico; Grand Turk, Turks & Caicos; Dominican Republic; Grand Cayman; Belize City, Belize; Cozumel, Mexico and return to Ft Lauderdale

On from Savannah! The second leg proceeded without incident and finally, touchdown at Lauderdale.

After parking and unloading in the general aviation area, Belinda went through the paperwork necessary to store the Otter as the Tigers taxied to a strong protective hangar. It wasn't hurricane season but they'd take no chances.

A large shuttle bus stood by for the travelers, ready to take them to the Port and the **SS *SOLARWIND***. A smaller jitney was available at the hangar to take the Flying Tigers to the ship after they concluded their shutdown operations.

The Flying Tiger Twins-Benedict and Galatea Tigris

A fleet of sparkling floating hotels ranging from huge to moderate size occupied all the available slips at Port Everglades. Glistening in the late afternoon sun, they had a fairy land aspect about them that reminded the Bear Twins of their recent trip to the Mystic Empire in Orlando. "Wow! Mom, Dad, Forget about buying a theme park. Let's buy one of these ships."

Octavius snorted, "Is there anything you two don't want to buy? Believe it or not, our resources do have limits. Let's see what Solar Seas has in store for us with their new sailing never-never land."

"Where is it?"

"Over there!'

"You mean the one with the weird looking towers?'

"Those weird looking towers are the wind and solar sails that help power and propel the ship. You guys wanted an ergonomically positive trip. This is how they do it."

The bus rolled up to the **SS *SOLARWIND***'s VIP gangway where they were met by several members of the crew. A sharply uniformed female fox greeted them. "Doctor Bear, Bearoness, members of the Octavian party. Welcome! I'm Commander Freddi Fox, the ship's social directress. We're so pleased you have chosen to join us a day early before the rest of the passengers arrive. We're delighted to have such a distinguished group on board. It's our aim to make your stay with us a sea-going delight. We have crew members standing by to take you all to your VIP suites on the Empire deck and help you get comfortably settled. Please step through our security check points and follow the stewards to the elevators. Dinner will be served shortly in several of the restaurants. Please call on us for whatever else you require."

Food! The Twins did fist bumps.

"Doctor Bear and Bearoness! The Captain would like to welcome you to the bridge as soon as you are available. Your entire party is invited to join him at one of his several tables tomorrow evening. As you can imagine, we have a significant population of VIPs and reporters due on board for this, our inaugural cruise. While the Solar Seas Company has been in the tourism business for many years, **SS *SOLARWIND*** is our first totally environmentally compliant vessel. This is her maiden voyage."

Belinda responded, "Thank you, Commander. We are so looking forward to this cruise. We will be delighted to meet the Captain and other Officers and crew members just as soon as we get located and settled."

They trooped off after the stewards who were showing off and demonstrating the ship's features and locations of interest on the way to the suites on the Empire deck right above the bridge. The super large, forward-facing Imperial Suite was reserved for the Great Bear and Belinda with the Twins' adjoining suite next door. Frau Schuylkill and Colonel Wyatt Where, her mate, shared a royal suite. Maury*(me)* Howard and Otto were in a large three bedroom arrangement as were Bearyl, Bearnice and Madame Giselle. So were Lord David, Dancin' Dan and Jack the Jaguar. The Flying Tigers were in a twosome with room for one more. Each suite, in addition to the separate bedrooms, sported separate baths, walk in closets, a butler and butler's quarters, a large common room and a small kitchenette to say nothing of the balconies. Video, internet and 5G phone service went without saying.

31

The Twins summed it up, "Wow!! This is costing a fortune."

After the stewards acquainted them with their butlers and suite facilities, the tourists took brief refuge in the individual baths and got ready for dinner at two cafés specializing in either continental or island cuisine. Once underway, there would be 11 restaurants available for breakfast, lunch, dinner and day and night long buffets and snacks. Much to the Twins' chagrin, the pizza stations weren't open yet. Neither were the shoppes or casino. They'd be closed whenever they were in port.

Octavius and the Bearoness got acquainted with Carlos, their Catalan Sheepdog butler and then took an elevator down one deck to the bridge. They knocked on the door and were greeted by a Great Albatross wearing a deck officer's cap, a three stripe brassard and a sidearm under his elongated wing. "Hello! Can I help you?"

"Yes, we're Doctor Octavius Bear and Bearoness Belinda Bearnaise Bruin Bear (nee Black). We were invited to the bridge by the Captain."

"Ah yes, you're here with your famous Octavian group. You're legendary in protection and crime fighting circles. Please come in. I'm Dudley Diomede, Chief Security Officer for **SS SOLARWIND**. Let me introduce you around. Ladies and Gentlebeasts, please say hello to the world renowned scientist, industrialist and criminologist Doctor Octavius Bear and his lovely wife, theatrical star and Scottish resort owner, Bearoness Belinda."

"Here is our Executive Purser, Gillian Greyhound. She and her staff are responsible for all our finance, payroll and administration including the ship's cargo and passenger manifests, our supplies, hotel management, entertainment, food, beverages and the casino. We call her our Hotelier Plus."

The svelte female dog smiled at the pair and said. "Welcome. I hope you have a wonderful stay with us. I've heard of Polar Paradise. I'd love to talk shop with you, Bearoness – one innkeeper to another."

Belinda laughed. "I'd invite you to bring the **SS SOLARWIND** to the Shetlands but I'm afraid our docking facilities are only large enough to accommodate the Abeardean ferries. This ship is magnificent."

"Thank you. Let me introduce you to our senior Deck Officers. This is First Officer Casimir, a Cashmere Goat." The goat looked up from making adjustments to the ship's control panels and saluted.

"This gentlebeast is Staff Captain Montmorency, a mongoose, second in command." He extended a paw to the visitors.

Octavius shook it and said, "I must introduce you to my executive assistant, Mauritius Meerkat. He's here with us. You two may have common ancestors."

The mongoose bowed in acknowledgement. Gillian Greyhound continued: "And now, the Grand Finale, our Captain and Master of the **SS SOLARWIND**, Lincoln Lion."

A white peaked cap profusely decorated with gold 'scrambled eggs' and nautical insignia sat atop a tall, muscular Panthera Leo's mature head and face. His brawny shoulders bore epaulettes with 4½ stripes surmounted by a gold loop. He strode across the bridge extending his paw in greeting.

"Bearoness and Doctor Bear, welcome aboard. Delighted you and your party decided to join us. Captain Lincoln Lion at your service. Yes, I am a Sea Lion." He guffawed. "Several of our officers are out and about through the ship - Our Chief Medical Officer, our Chief Engineer, our Safety Officer and our Environmental Compliance Officer. As you well know, the **SS SOLARWIND** is designed and maintained to be state of the art in ecologically conforming systems. On that subject, I wonder if I could ask you to delay your dinner a little longer. I have something I wish to discuss with you."

Belinda giggled, "As you can tell, Captain. Both Octavius and I can afford to miss a meal or two."

"Oh, no. I'll have Commander Greyhound ensure you are well fed. Gillian, please see to it. Two delayed deluxe dinners with appropriate wine for our guests."

The Purser saluted and picked up a phone, no doubt giving orders to the kitchens and restaurant managers as well as to Carlos, the butler assigned to their suite.

The Captain smiled as only a lion can smile, lifted his paw and pointed toward a bulkhead door. "Let's meet in my office. Commanders Diomede and Greyhound, please join us."

The two bears proceeded ahead of the officers into a well-appointed room with large windows that looked out over the dock, gangways and boarding ramps. A large group of burly gorillas were loading a massive amount of material into the ship's cargo holds. Forklift after forklift zipped up and down the ramps under the supervision of an officer they had not met. He scanned each loader before allowing it to enter the storage spaces and directed the empty outgoing hoists back onto the pier to pick up another full palette. The dance was fascinating.

The captain cleared his throat and settled behind a desk covered with electronic communications and computing devices. A small brass anchor was the only decorative touch.

He grinned and rumbled, "What's that they say in the business videos? 'I suppose you're wondering why I have called you all here.'"

Octavius, suspecting an upcoming situation, said, "Yes, Captain. I confess you have our attention."

"Doctor Bear! I'm afraid your Octavian group's reputation has preceded you and the Solar Sea Company wishes to employ you on a detective mission for this vessel. Some anonymous forces regard our ergonomic advances as dangers to the economics of the tourism industry. We have been threatened by email with harassment and serious damage."

"Oh no," thought Bel. "Here we go again."

She looked at the lion. "My husband and I are no longer active in crime fighting, Captain. We are retiring. That's why we're on your ship. To enjoy some long desired leisure."

"We understand but your band of experts is still functioning. We want to hire them. It's essential that we sail tomorrow as scheduled. Forgive me – with or without you two investigating. You would both be tremendous assets but I appreciate your desire to relax and get on with your lives."

Octavius nodded. "Thank you, but I guess I don't understand. Surely you have other options. Commander Diomede! You have a substantial security apparat at your disposal and Commander Greyhound, could you not delay departure until your security and safety teams get to the bottom of this?"

The Purser responded, "Doctor Bear, surely a highly successful executive such as yourself can appreciate the tremendous loss the company would incur if we don't fulfill our cruising obligations on schedule. Passenger lawsuits and massive refunds; ruined perishable food and beverages; extra fuel and maintenance to keep the ship's operations running;"

"We can't just shut down. Lost sales in the shoppes, restaurants and services. A major payroll hit! Overtime for 1200 permanent employees. Arbitration and union issues with our contract entertainers, vendors and transients; missed assignments and connections at our ports of call; extra costs here at Port Everglades. Do you have any idea what dockage fees are like? No! Threats or no threats, we have to sail on time." The Captain growled and agreed.

The Chief Security Officer took up the challenge. "You're correct, Doctor Bear, that I'm in charge of a large security staff and safety unit. But there's not a detective among them, including me."

"We maintain law and order. We have a brig but will use it sparingly. As with all cruisers, we deal with stowaways, contraband, drugs, unruly passengers and sometimes crew, drunks galore, missing kids, husbands, wives and relatives, mishaps, fires, deaths, casino issues. Our doctors treat medical problems and incidents. We're police and first responders. We do a damn good job of it. Our protection record on other ships has been excellent. But we're not trained or experienced investigators. If needed, we employ outside detective forces. We could use your team."

Octavius replied. "Did you say the top management of Solar Seas will be on board as well as a large group of reporters? Over a thousand passengers in all classes? I understand the exposures the company will sustain as a result of delays but what happens if these mysterious parties succeed in their harassment? Sabotage, an on board fire, dead in the water at sea, tainted food, equipment failure, accidents, even deaths."

"We're aware. That's what we want you to find and prevent. The company will directly compensate your team members if they are willing to participate."

Bel stared at Octavius. He shrugged. "Let me discuss it with the team. I'll be back to you in the morning or will you be otherwise engaged taking on passengers? We leave tomorrow evening, do we not?"

The Captain frowned. "Yes, we do. Threats or no threats. Stop up at the bridge as soon as you can in the morning. I'll call my crew together."

"Meanwhile so will I"

Chapter Three

SOLARWIND is a ship under threat
Although nothing untoward's happened yet
Will the Great Bear agree
To inquire and see
Who's the fish he can snare in his net?

Back at their suite, the two bears dug into a sumptuous meal laid before them by Carlos. They had checked to make sure the other Octavians had already been properly fed at the ship's open restaurants. The Twins were engaged in going back for thirds in the Italian trattoria.

Octavius looked at the Catalan Sheepdog butler and asked, "Carlos, Is this your first cruise for Solar Seas?"

"Oh no, Senor Bear, I have been employed by the company for several years. On the Seabright and Ocean Wanderer. Of course, this is my first cruise on this ship. It's her-how you say-damsel sailing."

Belinda smiled, "I think you mean 'maiden voyage'"

He laughed, "Oh, sí, sí, maiden voyage. She is an unusual ship, is she not? With the sun and wind sail towers. Like the big old galleons. We're going back in history. Of course, they didn't use the sun then, Just the wind."

"How do the crew members feel about this ship?"

"I do not know all of them, of course, but many of us are proud to be part of something new in cruising. Some of the ships got boring. However, a few of the old timers are upset. They don't trust the new sun sails and wind turbines or the new engines. They think we're going to be stranded in the middle of the ocean. I understand we have conventional engines and fuel as we may need it."

Belinda nodded, "That's what we've been told and of course the SS **SOLARWIND** went through extensive sea trials and a shakedown run. I hope all the bugs have been shaken out."

"Oh, Madame, there are no bugs on this vessel. Our cleaning crews wouldn't stand for it."

"No, no! I meant problemas, dificultades. Those kind of bugs"

"Oh! Aha! I see. Excuse me. I must refresh the suite's bathrooms."

As soon as he left, Octavius took up his laptop "Ursula, I assume you have been listening to all the discussions we've been having with the Captain and his officers."

"Yes, Doctor Bear, Do you plan to agree to his request?"

"That depends on what the Octavians think. Would you contact all of them and ask them to meet in my suite tomorrow at 9 after breakfast."

"Shall I include the Twins?"

"I'll never hear the end of it if I don't. Also, if we all agree to take on this problem, I want Chita involved. Call her and tell her to stand by, prepared to fly out to meet this ship at Nassau, our first stop."

"She didn't want to come. She won't be happy."

"As soon as she discovers there's possible dirty doings going on, she'll be right in her element. Madame Catt hates water but she loves crime. How about doing some research in the meantime?"

"That's right in my element. What am I looking for?"

"There are some cruise companies who object to the LNG and wind-solar propulsion this ship is using. If it succeeds, they'll be faced with immense pressure to retrofit or scrap their dirty HFO - based engines and engage in highly expensive ship refurbishments. Profits down the drain. I want to know what's going on in the industry. Who's protesting? Who's irate enough to threaten Solar Seas and follow through on those threats?"

"Just what my AI algorithms and circuits were designed for. I'll also contact Condo, Byzz and the Hex Deep Data mavens and see what I can uncover. Is tomorrow soon enough?"

Belinda gulped in amazement. "That would be lovely, Ursula dear. By the way, how many of you are there with our group?"

"Eight but I can summon up more."

"No, I think eight will be sufficient for the moment."

Chapter Four

Are the travelers willing to play?
It's left up to each member to say.
The Great Bear won't insist
But the gang can't resist.
The Octavians give their okay.

Belinda and Octavius were just finishing off the splendid breakfast Carlos had put before them and were downing the last contents of their bowls of coffee when they heard a knock on the door of their palatial suite. The butler beat them to the entrance and opened the door. "Good Morning, Carlos is it? I'm Maury Meerkat and these are my associates. Reporting for duty."

The steward looked questioningly at Octavius and Belinda. "It's fine, Carlos. They're our Octavian gang and we asked them to come by. Perhaps a little coffee. Enough for 17 if we have that many bowls." He left for the kitchenette, shaking his head.

The group trooped through the entranceway into the suite's common area. Otto whistled. "I thought I had a posh set of digs but this is fantastic." He turned to Octavius. "We're guessing but the consensus is you have an assignment for us. There go our vacations."

The Great Bear laughed. "Only if you're interested. It shouldn't take up much of your time." He proceeded to outline the Captain's request and was besieged with a torrent of questions.

"Do we have any clue as to who the culprits could be?"

"Not yet. Ursula's on the job."

"What do we do if we find them?"

"The Cruise company will deal with them."

"There's slightly more than a thousand animals coming on board today. It could be anybody or anything. Even somebody not on the ship. A collision, malware hackers, pirates, terrorists or worse. "

"Right! Are we up for it?

Maury *(Me)*, the Colonel, Frau, Otto, Howard, the Flying Tigers, Jack, Lord David and Dan all agreed. Giselle, Bearyl and Bearnice were dubious but went along. The twins were ecstatic. More grist for their electronic games. The new *Bears in Space* was out and now *Bears at Sea* was in the works. Belinda shrugged. Retirement was elusive.

"OK," said the Great Bear, "I'll go to the Captain and take on his commission. Bel and I will also participate. No way we're staying out of this. After all, we're passengers on this ship, too. If something happens, we'll be involved. Maury, Colonel, Frau Ilse, and Howard. Join Bel and me on the bridge. Otto, I know you and Mlle Woof have to rehearse for the Welcome Aboard Show. I'll brief the rest of you afterwards. I don't want to overwhelm them with the whole team but you'll all be in on the action." He looked at the Twins and grinned. "You too."

Ursine high fives! "Carlos, do you have anything to eat?"

Maury here: "Once more unto the breach, dear friends, once more;" I doubt Henry the Fifth was ever on a cruise ship but he had the right idea or at least Will Shakesbear did. "The game's afoot." (I'll bet you thought Sherlock Holmes came up with that one. Nope! It was good old Henry V by way of the Bard.)

Our small mob of 6 approached the bridge. Octavius knocked on the door and was admitted by a female greyhound officer who was on her way out. "Oh, Doctor Bear, Lady Belinda! I'm going down to the gangways. The first wave of passengers is on its way over from the terminal building. We check them in there and then direct them to the correct ship portal along with their luggage. Commander Diomede is down there supervising entries. Can you tell me what you've decided?"

The Great Bear turned to the four newbies and said, "This is the ship's Executive Purser, Commander Gillian Greyhound. She's in charge of the business and hotel side of the **SS *SOLARWIND***. Commander, these are my top detectives among the Octavians. There's one more, a cheetah, who will be joining us in Nassau. The entire team of 17 including the Bearoness and myself will be at your disposal."

40

"Excellent. I'm sure the Captain will be pleased. Please go in. Dudley and I will catch up with you after we handle the incoming surge. Fortunately, since this is our first commercial voyage, we didn't have to manage debarking passengers. It makes it much easier. Turnarounds can be a nightmare." She turned back inside. "Captain Lion! Doctor Bear, the Bearoness and some of the Octavians are here. They've agreed to take our case."

The skipper pumped his paws in the air and roared, shaking Otto and me. I expected the wolves and bears to roar back. They didn't. Howard made whatever noises porcupines normally make. "Wonderful, Octavius and Octavians. The company brass will be very pleased as am I. There will be several Captain's Welcome tables set up in the gourmet restaurants tonight. All of your party is invited to participate. Right now, the boarding process is beginning and my command team is up to their ears. That will be followed by final preparations for sail away this evening. We'll be underway to Nassau, our first port of call. *(Where we expect to meet Chita.)*. I hope nothing happens overnight. Let us all get together tomorrow morning first thing and share information, plot strategies and assign duties.

Octavius replied, "Thank you, Captain but we don't want to be idle for 24 hours. Would it be possible for us to tour the bridge and visit the engine room? They're probably the most vulnerable spots on the ship."

"Let me call Commander Pronghorn, our Chief Engineer and see what can be arranged." He picked up his radio and said, "Commander Pronghorn to the bridge, please." The Engineer acknowledged and responded, "On my way, Sir."

The Captain turned to a mongoose, Staff Captain Montmorency, his second in command and said, "Monty, the ship is yours for the next hour or so while I get these folks set up with Pruitt Pronghorn and a tour of the propulsion units. Oh, let me introduce you to Doctor Bear's number one, Mr. Mauritius Meerkat."

I shook the Staff Captain's paw and said, "We're not exactly the same species but close enough. Small as we are, our fate seems to be tied to supporting large fearsome animals."

"Too true but I really enjoy cruising. I assume you like detecting."

I replied. "You bet but I'm also a theatrical agent and author. Several members of our party are booked in your theater and show lounges. We have a Tarot and Magic show, dramatic readings by a famous Polar Actress and a singing gig by her Twin. We have lots of twins. Two Tigers who pilot our planes and of course, The Doctor's and Bearoness' children. I also write up Octavius' adventures."

"A regular Doctor Watson! Well, welcome aboard. I'll try get down to the show venues and catch your proteges. Ah, here comes the Chief Engineer."

A greying Pronghorn Deer came in shaking his head and mumbling. "Those damn elevators have to act up on boarding day. Passengers are backed up on the entry decks. Oh well! We're on it. You wanted me, Captain?"

"Yes Pruitt. I want you to meet Doctor Octavius Bear and some of his associates. They're VIP guests but they are also famous detectives and experienced crime fighters. They've agreed to look into those anonymous threats we've been receiving."

Introductions, paw and hoof shakes all around.

The Engineer said, "Glad you're going to work on it. The ship's propulsion, electrical and power support units are my babies and that's where we're highly vulnerable. Only our communications, computing, navigation and control systems are more worrisome. We have a top notch team of technical support mavens charged with keeping the bridge, internet, passenger rooms, video, external and internal phone and radio service operating. Places like the kitchens, restaurants, shoppes, sick bay, gyms, spas, theatres, swimming pools all need constant attention. The sails and wind turbines have their own service staff. Of course, there's the almighty Casino. Damn place can drive you nuts. And now the elevators have hiccups."

The Great Bear replied. "Right now, we'd like to visit the engine room."

"Engine rooms! There's three of them and four separate battery rooms. The computer servers are in several venues. Tell you what. Give me an hour to see about these elevators and set up a tour for you. I'll meet you down at the Deck Zero portal at 10:30."

"Fine! I'll gather my team and we'll make our way below."

The Pronghorn went over to speak to the Staff Captain for few moments and then headed out. Captain Lion said, "I have to go down and do some meet and greet duty. As you can imagine, the maiden voyage of the **SS SOLARWIND** has the top brass of the company coming on board to observe, supervise, suggest, wine and dine and report. Hopefully, not to complain or fire anybody, especially me. They'll probably hit the Casino once we're in international waters. With any luck, they'll debark in Nassau."

"We also have a flock of reporters wanting to file stories on this new 'wondership'. They definitely will wine, dine and gamble. Commander Greyhound and our social directress, Commander Fox will have their paws full."

"Finally we have the VIP Old Faithfuls, repeat customers of Solar Seas who want to experience the new vessel. They'll no doubt want to tour the ship, meet the Captain, dine at the Captain's tables and schmooze with the Company bigwigs. They too, will have plenty of opinions and reactions."

"Doctor Bear, can you and your team help with the socializing? You're all famous. We won't tell the reporters or the return voyagers about your detective assignment. You're all here to get some well-deserved R&R. But the Solar Seas executives who know about the threats will want to meet and question you. I'm sure your delightful wife and other members of the Octavians such as the lovely Frau here will be able to charm, soothe and distract them."

Octavius was a bit put off by the prospect and looked at his team with a raised eyebrow. They grinned back. Maybe he and Giselle could do personal Tarot card readings. Oh well, Solar Seas will be paying for their services. He reluctantly agreed.

"OK, Captain! Although this wasn't what we had in mind when we decided to take a cruise. Maury, see if you can find the Twins. A trip to the engine rooms is right down their alley. The Flying Tigers, Jaguar Jack and Lord David will probably be interested, too. Otto and Giselle are busy. A shame Chita isn't here. Staff Captain Montmorency, can you describe the bridge and show us its instruments, controls, devices and technology while we're here?"

"I'll be happy to. Actually there are three bridges: center, port and starboard. Instrument and control-wise they are complete duplicates. As you can imagine, the outboard bridges are essential for docking or maneuvering in tight spaces like a canal or river."

Maury (me) returned with the Twins in tow, goggle eyed and mesmerized. The Flying Tigers were with them. "I couldn't find Jack or David.:"

The Staff Captain waved. "Hi, Kids. Join us!"

"Wow! The Bridge! Where's the big wooden ship's wheel?"

"There isn't any. That small aircraft size wheel is it."

"Oh sure, electronics. But where are all the screens?

"We use heads-up displays. On the windows on all three bridges.

"Like on fighter planes?"

"Right! Obviously we rely on a number of instruments and technologies ranging from GPS and radar to depth soundings, engine settings and performance, fuel management, solar and wind mast placement, azipod and thruster positions and electronic charting. And of course, weather reports. Computers, computers, computers! The ship can run on autopilot over a plotted course but the bridge officers are there to make sure the wind and tides haven't thrown us off."

"What are azipods?"

They propel and steer the ship. Envision propellers attached to pods that can swivel 360° (that's the azi part) positioned at the bow, stern and midships of the vessel. They're on each side - both port and starboard.

Thrusters are what the name suggests. They expel gasses and water. Most of them are fixed in direction. In combination, azipods and thrusters move us forward and backward, make turns and hold us stationary. Very handy for docking, steering around port traffic, and negotiating obstacles like sand bars and wrecks."

Galatea remarked, "I assume all your computers are well backed up."

"Oh yes, in triplicate on board and in the Cloud. Our computers are remotely managed and updated from Solar Seas headquarters over satellites. Have our Chief Engineer show you our server clusters. State of the art!"

Octavius interrupted. "Speaking of whom. It's time for us to go down to the engine rooms and meet Commander Pronghorn."

The Staff Captain frowned. "I hope they fixed the glitches on the elevators. The incoming pax (passengers) aren't going to like climbing stairs unless they're exercise freaks. Let me check for you."

His paws flew over his keyboard. "They seem to be operating OK. Pruitt and his staff score again. Thank him for me when you see him on Deck Zero."

Benedict said, "More computer controls. I guess the passenger registration system and the cabin door key cards are all linked."

"Oh yes and your key card can be used in the shoppes, spas, restaurants, bars, the casino, events and shows, even lounge chairs on the Lido deck."

"So most of the time you know where a passenger is?"

"It's not Big Brother but it does help with security and safety and of course, billing at departure. We've occasionally had a passenger go missing for a while on other ships. Often it's kids. Thank goodness we don't allow pets on board although the Purser has a puppy. Don't tell anyone!"

"Well, thank you, Staff Captain."

"Call me Monty."

"And I'm Octavius and this is Bel. I assume we'll be seeing more of each other as we investigate these threatening emails. Have you seen them?"

"Yep! Vague but definitely menacing. Not sure what's intended. The Captain has them. I hope you get to the bottom of this."

"We'll do our best. Do you have any suggestions?"

"It's somebody on this ship. An unhappy crew member or someone who is being paid to cause panic."

"Any names?"

"No, and it's definitely not me." He laughed. "I don't think it's any of the Deck Staff. Possibly some animal on the Hotel side. Unfortunately there's a mob of them at all levels. Some of them aren't paid much and they might have seen a way to supplement their earnings. The plus side is most of them wouldn't know how to inflict damage other than in their own bailiwicks."

"But some of those bailiwicks like the kitchens could cause a major disaster."

"True. Commanders Greyhound and Diomede have their work cut out for them."

"And now, us too. Thanks Staff Captain. On to those temperamental elevators. Engine rooms, here we come."

McTavish asked. "Before we go, can we blow the ship's horn?"

"Why not? Here, Go ahead!"

BLAAAAT!! BLAAAAT!!

"Oh, wow! That was great!"

The Development of Civilization Volume 18
Part 3
Cruise Ships - Power and Propulsion
From "An Introduction to Faunapology"
by Octavius Bear Ph.D.

As mentioned earlier, cruise ships are floating hotels, often massive in size making lengthy voyages. They are ravenous consumers of fuel needed to satisfy all the requirements of their numerous passengers and to propel them over their often long and complex sea-routes. Unfortunately, they are notorious polluters, with a few exceptions we've previously touched on. They can't shut down while docked. Well over half of their power is consumed in motion or moorage. The rest supports all the hotel services and amenities at sea or at rest. All in all, they are power hogs.

Faced with gigantic expenses and pressure from governments and environmentalists, the industry has been making efforts to improve the situation in several ways:

Fuel: Substituting Liquefied Natural Gas (LNG) for sulphur laden Heavy Fuel Oil (HFO). Unfortunately LNG is more expensive, requires special handling and storage and engine modification.

Power Supplements: A few ships have been developed or modified to use wind and solar devices to augment their conventional propulsion and electrical generation capabilities. They are still on many drawing boards, expensive and requiring a new set of crew skills to manage and maintain. There are also emerging techniques for using local power when docked. Scrubbers and particle precipitators are being used increasingly to cut back on airborne pollution. More water and solid wastes are recycled.

What about nuclear? Great for navies. Possible for merchant ships. Not likely for cruisers. Passenger, public and governmental reaction is too negative and some believe that terrorists would attack the ships to capture the reactors. Don't frighten the tourists or the port authorities. Advanced cruise ship power could be a long and troubling voyage.

Chapter Five

What is making the SOLARWIND go?
The Octavians all want to know.
Do the winds and the sun
Help the huge engines run?
The response is a definite "No"

The Chief Engineer met us outside the Deck Zero passenger elevator door. With Octavius' girth, we had to make several trips to get all nine of us down there.

He chuckled, "Welcome to a totally different world. Luxury above. Utility below. I should have had you use the freight elevators. Thank goodness the lifts are working again. I didn't want to explain that to the Company's top brass."

"What was wrong with the elevators?"

"Computer glitch. The techies rebooted and we're good to go."

"Does that happen often?"

"Hardly ever. I don't really understand it but elevator maintenance isn't my strong suit. By the way, I think the Captain got another email. I don't know what it said. He'll tell you later. Right now, he and the Purser, Social Directress. PR Manager and Security Chief are up to their ears socializing with executives, reporters and VIP guests. Better them than me. That's why I prefer it here belowdecks. Anyway, One guided tour coming up."

Deck Zero was actually several levels high and stretched from prow to stern. Floor to ceiling bulkheads divided the spaces separating the two primary engines, the solar and wind generators, the drive shafts for the azipods and blowers for the thrusters. Three rooms housed the ship's profusion of batteries. The heavily insulated Liquefied Natural Gas tanks also acted as ballast and sat atop the keel below the deck. The ship has a double bottom hull, and a cofferdam between tanks. *(Necessary! A break below the waterline could leak methane. Anyway, I'm not a naval architect.)* All of them were kept apart to reduce the impact of flood, fire or leakages of all kinds. Several offices and utility/tool rooms on the deck supported the crew. Anchor chains ran down through separate isolated compartments.

What was missing were the hellish furnaces that characterized the steamships of the past. But the engines, motors and generators threw off some heat and still made significant noise as they poured power to the thousands of hungry devices and outlets in the decks above and moved the ship on its course.

The computer and cable rooms were on Deck One above. The client server computers took up most of the available space on that level. Rooms for the technicians and the technology officers filled out the remaining bays.

The engineer continued, "The *SOLARWIND* is powered by a much cleaner combination of solar panels, wind power and liquid natural gas, and should produce 40% less carbon dioxide than a traditional cruise ship. Sun and wind provide electricity. LNG moves the ship. She has a maximum speed of 21 knots and a cruising speed of 17 knots. Not bad for a floating hotel."

"We have a solar farm on the top deck. It incorporates a self-sustained garden that uses recycled garbage and wastewater. The closed-loop water use system uses rainwater, wastewater and seawater to irrigate the plants, many of which end up in our kitchens."

"The heating and air-conditioning are augmented by the recycled waste energy, taken from the main engine, and will reduce electricity load by 50%. Altogether, we're getting maximum use out of our rubbish resources."

The Octavians were goggle-eyed. The Twins said, "Let's build one of these, Dad. UUI ENVIRONMENTALS. A new division."

"You're talking billions, Son. Maybe a partnership, we'll see."

Arabella giggled. "We'll call it the Ocko-Eco Partner Ship." McTavish guffawed and Howard smiled. The wolves chortled and wagged their capacious tails. Belinda laughed and shrugged. I chuckled. Octavius didn't.

The Pronghorn grinned and said, "You guys think big. Speaking of big, let's take a look at the engines." He led us through a bulkhead door into a chamber of mechanical noise. These engines are actually steam turbines using LNG boil off but can also use diesel if necessary. But maybe I'm getting too technical. Bottom line they're highly efficient."

The Frau shook her head. "They're also very big."

"It's a big ship."

Octavius turned and said. "Thank you, Commander Pronghorn. This is quite a world you live in. I'd like to see the computers in the server farm on the next deck. Back in Kentucky we have a huge facility that powers our Advanced Super Computing Center in the Deep Data Hexagon. I'd like to compare."

"Sure, let's go. We'll use the stairs. Faster than waiting for elevators for a one deck climb. I hope they're still working. I saw a Solar Seas chopper descending on the helipad when I came down here. The Execs have arrived. The Captain doesn't want to have to explain stuck elevators. Neither do I."

"I thought you said they were fixed?"

"I sure hope so! Computers and elevators are an unruly bunch."

We entered a large, darkened space – an extensive server room filled with computers, routers, power supplies, cables, and related electronics on 19-inch racks. The Pronghorn chuckled. "You just saw the **SOLARWIND's** muscles. Here are the brains."

McTavish looked around. "It's not the Hex but what is? Bella, somewhere in there *The Bold Brave Brilliant Bumptious Bears* and *Bears in Space* are zipping away. Maybe while we're on this ship, we can work on *Bears at Sea*."

The Colonel said, "There's a lot more running in here besides games although I suppose the Casino is a heavy user."

The Engineer snorted. "That damn money hole chews up more bytes and cycles than most of the rest of the ship. And it's not even functioning at the moment. We have to be outside the twelve mile limit. When I was a young fawn my mother taught me Pronghorn games. We never had those slot machines - clanging monstrosities that chew up your money and spit back pennies. Actually, with ship credit cards, there's no actual cash moving around at all. Just tons of electrons. And we have to supply it. Oh well! It's a job. Anyway, this concludes our tour, Ladies and Gentlebeasts. I hope I didn't bore you.

He was greeted with enthusiastic applause. He bowed and escorted us to the freight elevator that would take us up to the promenade deck and outdoor restaurants. Predictably, the Twins were fascinated and famished.

McTavish *(as usual)* enthused mightily. "This ship is fantastic. Do you suppose we could see the solar and wind masts in action. Spinning sails. They lower them to go under a bridge. That must be something to see. Anyway, what I'd like to see right now is lunch."

Agreement all around.

Chapter Six

The executives of Solar Seas
From the President to the VPs
Arrive on launch day,
All enthused to display
Their tropical cruise expertise.

The restaurants were filling up as more and more passengers came onboard. The Octavians picked a seafood grill and took up several tables. Just as Octavius and Belinda were about to be seated, the ship's Social Directress, Freddi Fox, came over to their table and said, "Hello, Doctor Bear and Bearoness. I've been searching for you. Our executives arrived by chopper a while ago and the Captain would like to introduce you and invite you to join them for lunch. They're in a closed-off room further forward on this deck. Please come with me. Feel free to bring a couple of members of your Octavian team."

The Great Bear nodded and beckoned Howard and me to join Belinda and him. We followed Freddi to a nondescript door not far from the bridge. The interior was hardly nondescript. In a space clearly dedicated to business meetings, paneled in walnut and distressed brick, with a podium and several large screens a small group sat at two long tables set for a conference meal. Bottles of white and red wine were spaced evenly among the delicate chinaware dishes and sparkling crystal. All eyes concentrated on the four animals entering the room.

Captain Lion rose and waved in welcome, pointing to four empty seats. The social directress smiled and said, "Gentlebeasts. May I present Doctor Octavius Bear and The Bearoness Belinda Bearnaise Bruin Bear. Mr. Mauritius Meerkat and Doctor Howard Watt are members of the Octavian group. I must return to the checking in process below which I'm happy to say, is going quite smoothly." She looked away from the Captain and over to the Maitre d,' a uniformed ferret and said, "I'll leave you in Wilhelm's capable hands." She withdrew from the room.

Before the captain could say anything, a large, fully antlered Elk stood, bugled and said, "I'm Wally Wapiti, CEO of Solar Seas. Welcome! Let me introduce our Chief Operating Officer, Coleman Cougar; Bill Beaver,

Senior Vice President for Sales and Marketing; our CFO, Loretta Lynx; Corporate Attorney Emilia Emu and Corporate Security Officer Pablo Puma. I'm aware of you as a scientist and industrialist, Doctor Bear. UUI-Universal Ursine Industries isn't it? I didn't know you're also an experienced criminologist with a staff of detectives. The Captain just enlightened me."

The CFO swiveled her head from Octavius to the Captain and back. "I don't understand why we're spending the money to employ this group of outsiders. Pablo, Captain Lion, surely our Corporate and Ship Security should be capable of handling an issue like this. It's probably a hoax, anyway. Why are we hiring them?"

The Great Bear reared up to his full nine foot height, almost hitting the ceiling. and huffed. "On the contrary, Madam. We are VIP passengers paying full freight on this vessel. We came on board intent on rest and relaxation. Now, we are responding to the Captain's request for assistance. Nothing would please me better than to turn this issue back to Solar Seas for resolution. My wife and I have retired and my staff has been overworked for a long time. We certainly don't need employment from your company." He moved toward the door.

The Elk intervened. "Loretta, the emails the captain has received are probably not a hoax. Our security staffs are quite good at what they do but they are not detectives. Those are the skills we need to cut this thing off before any issues arise. I agreed with Captain Lion to seek expertise that we don't have. An incident on the **SOLARWIND's** maiden voyage with a mob of reporters and repeat VIP customers on board would be disastrous not only for this ship but for Seven Seas' entire fleet. Please sit down, Doctor Bear and enjoy your lunch. You too, Bearoness and gentlebeasts."

Octavius returned to the table. "Thank you, Mr. Wapiti. We've already examined the bridge, the engine rooms and the computer center – all of which are potentially vulnerable. There are other places such as the kitchens, restaurants and casino that are next on our list. Captain, we have only heard of the threats second hand. We need to see the emails themselves. As soon as you, Commanders Diomede and

Greyhound can get loose from the boarding process, we must get together. Preferably before the ship leaves port. All of you are invited to join us but especially you, Mr. Puma. By the way, do you have relatives in Brazil?"

"Nope, my family's from New Mexico. Why do you ask?"

"We once had an incident with another Puma. Not a nice animal. Glad you're not related. *(See Book Two - The Case of the Spotted Band.)*

Bill Beaver, Senior VP for Sales and Marketing said, "I'd like to join you when you review the casino. Most animals believe we make mountains of money from gaming. Not so! Only 10 percent of our company's profit comes from shipboard wagering. We provide it primarily as a diversion and entertainment for our passengers. Most of the games are very low stakes and the electronic slot machines are the big attraction. Most passengers are gambling novices."

"As soon as the ship is outside the 12-mile limit, dealers, mostly women, provide classes at unused tables in card-playing, dice and roulette. We even provide a textbook, which the beginners are allowed to keep that explains the rules and techniques in simple language."

"The overhead is terrific. Fully staffed as it is now, the casino has some 60 employees, including the casino manager, three assistant managers, 10 supervisors and two or three slot machine repairmen and computer specialists. The jobs are in great demand despite marginal salaries. The dealers and croupiers count on pooled tips, which for the non-Americans who constitute most of the staff are usually tax-free. Dealers come from the UK, Canada, Chile, Colombia, Peru, Holland, the Bahamas and the U.S."

The Puma Security Officer joined in. "A closed circuit TV system records all that happens at the gaming tables. We can review the tapes if our suspicions are aroused. The slots have their own computer aided record keeping. The managers and supervisors pay pretty close attention. We have the occasional cheater or protester but generally, in spite of the infernal mechanical and animal noises, things are pretty calm."

Octavius said, "Thanks gentlebeasts. When the ship passes the 12 mile limit, we'll be down to the casino to look things over. Captain, this meal was delicious but when can we get together?"

"I should be wrapping up my stint at the boarding process in another hour. Let's say 4 o'clock. I'll call you with a location. I'll gather my administrative officers." He looked at the Elk. "Of course, Solar Seas management is quite welcome. Doctor Bear, I assume you want your entire team there. "

"Yes, I do. Please gather any communications you've gotten from your adversaries. We want to look for style, mistakes and anything else that might identify them."

"I'll get Staff Captain Mongoose to put it all together.

Octavius looked at me, winked and said. "Ask our friend to gather the troops at 4 PM and stand by to analyze the emails."

Of course, he meant Ursula. I winked back and went on to finishing my lunch under the skeptical eye of the CFO.

The COO and Corporate Attorney had kept their peace throughout the meal. The COO, Coleman Cougar, growled. "I hope we can head this off. The other ship lines would like nothing better than to see us embarrassed on *SOLARWIND's* first passenger voyage. The reporters will have a field day and the negative word of mouth from the VIPs and all the paxes will be devastating. What do you think, Emilia?"

The lawyer frowned, stretched her long neck and rustled her feathers. "Let's not jump to conclusions, Coleman, We haven't seen these threats. Loretta may be right. It may be a hoax designed to rattle our cages on Debut Day. On the other hand, we may end up awash in lawsuits. I'll have to take on extra staff and hire a couple of outside firms. Our CFO will go crazy at the expense, won't you Loretta.. I hope your team is as good as advertised, Doctor Bear."

"We don't advertise, Madam. We just respond. I've also recently had major legal issues to contend with thanks to attacks by a rogue Chief Technical Officer. He's no longer with us, thank goodness, but his impact lingers." *(See Book 14. The Case of Cosmic Chaos)*

Bill Beaver looked at the Great Bear. "So you have experience with this malware stuff."

"Oh indeed! We have a whole unit of experts dedicated to dealing with malware and ransomware. They are highly competent and are doing constant research and testing to stay ahead of the bad guys. While it's not at all certain, if it turns out we will be dealing with computer network attacks, I have the ability to call them in immediately. I hope that gives you some assurance, Ms. Emu."

The lawyer smiled. The CFO, on the other hand, twitched her whiskers, annoyed at being put in her place at least temporarily.

The Wapiti said, "That sounds very reassuring. Why don't we let Wilhelm here dazzle us with culinary delights. I certainly don't want to waste a gourmet lunch. We have a press conference slated for 2PM. Bearoness, I have seen you perform with your Aquabear troupe. Quite lovely and entertaining. Are you still doing shows?"

"Only on special occasions, Mr. Wapiti. The ladies and I are relaxing."

"Oh please, call me Wally."

She gave him her thousand watt smile and said, "And I am Belinda."

The Emu and Lynx looked like they would like to choke.

*****

2PM and members of the press corps were directed by Freddi and Ernie Ermine, the ship's PR Director into a large conference room. Twenty five reporters, columnists, TV and Podcast Journalists and their associated sound technicians, photographers and videographers took up positions in front of a podium on which was emblazoned the **SOLARWIND's** logo. Ernie was handing out slick brochures and information sheets to each participant while Freddi was seeing about soft drinks and coffee bowls.

The Captain, Purser and Deck Commanders were seated up front opposite the Solar Seas management. Solar Seas President and CEO, Wally Wapiti stepped to the podium.

"Ladies and Gentlebeasts of the Press. Welcome to the next generation of ecologically responsible cruising: the **SS SOLARWIND.** I am Wally Wapiti, the CEO of Solar Seas Cruise Lines. We are very proud of this wonderful vessel and delighted to have you aboard to help us celebrate her maiden voyage. Let me introduce my dryland executives and then I will ask Captain Lion to join me at the podium to introduce his outstanding Group of Officers and to participate in a Q&A session." *(Introductions and Referrals)*

"You have handouts with the crew's and our executive's bios; all of the ship's specifications, **SOLARWIND's** cruise itineraries for the next year and a list of all our amenities, sports, entertainments, facilities, service, accommodations and of course food and drink. *(Laughs)* I hope your accommodations exceed your expectations. We have also provided descriptions of our shore excursions at each of our Ports of Call. I understand that most of you will be leaving us in San Juan. So am I. I hope that's enough time for you to experience the charms and excitement of this truly unique and advanced vessel. Now, I don't want to keep you from the shuffleboard courts. *(Laughs)* but are there any questions you'd like to address to us.

A wizened turkey TV producer asked, "How much did it cost to build and operate this marvel and how much do you charge per passenger per cruise?"

Purser Greyhound answered. "In the order you asked, $700 million to build, About 300 million to operate. Including agency and port fees; Onboard expenses; Payroll; Food; Fuel and other operating expenses. Passenger charges vary by level and yes, we do make a profit."

Wally smiled and said, "Thank you all for coming. We'll be available over the next few days." End of Conference.

Chapter Seven

The threat messages are shown to all
But the Captain refuses to stall.
"Let the terrorist do what he can.
This ship's leaving according to plan.
On to Nassau, our first port of call."

Another session. The Captain arranged for a conference suite and Ursula had passed the location on to our troops. Everyone was there at 4 PM. The ship was due to leave port at 5. Madame Giselle, Sir Otto, Bearyl and Bearnice finished up their rehearsals for the Welcome Aboard show. The Twins were their hyper selves. The Flying Tigers, Frau Schuylkill, Colonel Where and Howard entered the room. Jaguar Jack, Lord David and Dancing Dan came down from the Lido deck with tropical drinks in their paws. And of course, Octavius, Bel and I were front and center. Several covert versions of Ursula 15 and 16 were spread around the room on laptops.

On the **SOLARWIND** side, the Captain, Purser, Security Chief, Engineer and PR Manager were seated at a table next to several video screens and a PC.

The Solar Seas Company Brass were in full attendance, even the suspicious CFO Loretta Lynx.

Captain Lincoln Lion kicked the session off. "Thank you all for coming. The topic is the warnings. All of the threats we have received have been in the form of emails. Am I correct, Mr. Puma, that Corporate has not received any missives?"

Pablo Puma nodded.

"There have been six in all, spread over two weeks. The last one came in several hours ago." He pressed a key on the computer.

Six terse messages appeared on the screens. Ship's Security Chief Diomede commented. "Before you ask, we checked the sending addresses. All different and all phonies. No signatures."

The electronic posts read:

1. (Dated two weeks ago.) "You spent a lot of money on that ecological monster. You're about to spend a lot more."

2. (Two days later.) "Scrap your launch plans or else."

3. (Two more days) "You'll be sorry!"

4. (Another two days) "You've been warned!"

5. (Two days ago) "This is your last notice. Don't sail!"

6. (Today) "You're boarding reporters, VIPs and over a thousand paying passengers. You've passed the point of no return. Get ready for disaster."

The Great Bear snorted. "Well, whoever it is, they've been on the ship or watching it closely. My money is on a crew member or vendor. Has any member of the crew debarked in the last few hours? Are you still taking on supplies?"

Dudley Diomede answered. "I don't think so but I'll check our entry and exit records." He keyed into his personal laptop,

The Purser asked. "We scan all the incoming baggage. Could someone have gotten a bomb or other device on board past security?"

Pablo Puma said, "Those scanners are very efficient. The port hires out sniffer dogs and we use them, too. Who and What did we catch?"

Dudley replied. "Marijuana, heroin, cocaine, fentanyl, 20 bottles of liquor, 3 guns, 1 pet cat – all back on the dock along with their owners. No bombs. All crew members present and accounted for when we sealed the gangways. Same for the vendors who run the art gallery, some shoppes, auction site and dance studios. Any crew member or merchant who belongs is still on board."

Howard said, "The messages are too short to get much out of them but they seem to be coming from the same source."

Octavius stood up. "OK, Captain, Mr. Wapiti, we'll see what else we can find out. I assume you still intend to sail."

The Captain looked at the Elk who nodded. "We leave port at 5."

Chapter Eight

Off she goes with a showy farewell,
And she plows through the great Ocean's swell.
Down Caribbean ways
For the next fourteen days.
Of her future. Ask Madame Giselle!

At exactly 5 PM, the ship's horn echoed over the Port Everglades Cruise slips. Two short speeches by the Solar Seas President and the Mayor of Ft. Lauderdale. "First ship of its kind. Godspeed!"

When Wally Wapiti strode back up the last remaining gangway, it was withdrawn and the dockside crew released the mooring hawsers. The Solar Seas Company's **SOLARWIND** moved slowly out of her berth to the cheers of the passengers and crew and the dock-based observers. A Coast Guard cutter and two fireboats stood by in the channel amid a collection of small boats. Overhead a press helicopter and several drones captured the event. The ship blew its horn repeatedly. The Octavians stood on their balconies as the pilot and bridge officers negotiated a careful dance past the other cruise vessels, some of which were preparing to make their own exits toward the ocean.

As the ship headed through the channel leading to the open waters of the North Atlantic a frenzy of activity seized the crew, observers and passengers alike. The fireboats released two arcing water streams in salute. The traditional streamers and fireworks floated over the water. We watched the receding shoreline as the **SOLARWIND** turned into the Atlantic heading south to the Caribbean and the Bahamas, first stop on the island-hopping run. Nassau was only 164.29 nautical miles away, an early morning arrival. Hopefully, Chita would be waiting after her flight from London.

Back to suites and cabins, dressing for dinner at 6. The Octavians were invited to Captain's tables in several of the poshest restaurants. They would join the Solar Seas executives and the cruise line's VIP Old Faithful regulars. At 8, they would make their way to reserved seats in The Caribbean Theater for the *Welcome Aboard SOLARWIND* show.

Belinda was loaded down with her bearonial jewels. Octavius, as usual, had to fight his way into a tuxedo and formal shirt and tie with an assist from Howard and the Frau. She was also decked out in tasteful attire and ornaments. The Colonel was in dress uniform. The Twins, surprisingly, togged up. No doubt, they learned how from their interplanetary voyages and their trip Down Under. They and I were seated with their parents in the exclusive Gourmet Gardens along with the Solar Seas brass and a group of VIPs. Madame Giselle, Sir Otto, Bearyl and Bearnice, all in their show biz outfits were joined by the Flying Tigers and the Polar Paradise trio in the nearby Solar Seas Room along with some VIPs and the ship's off-duty officers.

Freddi Fox and PR manager Ernest Ermine were in hyper-schmooze mode, leading the Old Faithfuls to their tables in all three rooms, chatting them up and asking about their needs and requirements. They made special mention of the exciting features of the Welcome Aboard show and introduced the world famous performers in the Solar Seas room.

Mrs. Gladys Vaquero, a pretentious overdressed heifer was vociferously complaining that they were not seated in the Gourmet Gardens and were stuck together with the 'hired help'. Giselle smiled at her and made a note to call her up during her act and give her a negative prediction from the Tarot. Her husband, Humphrey, a grizzled bull and Texas oil billionaire, was loudly explaining to all comers how the ship's solar and wind sails worked and what they did. Of course, he had it all wrong but the officers weren't going to correct him. The two bovines had obviously hit the cocktail bars enthusiastically before making their appearance at the table.

Captain Lion started making his rounds in the Gourmet Gardens and asked Wally Wapiti, Octavius and the Bearoness to join him. The Elk, with well-polished antlers, was all welcoming grace. The Bears were introduced to the VIPs as the fabulous Polar swimming and film star and member of Scottish nobility and her equally famous husband, giga-billionaire, scientist and industrialist. No mention of criminology or detection. He moved impressively erect at his nine foot height. As they passed among the tables, the CEO murmured, "Any news?"

Octavius shook his head and murmured back. "Nothing yet. I still think it's a passenger or crew member. We're watching. Let's hope we get to Nassau unscathed."

The Elk snorted, "Let's hope we finish the cruise unscathed."

Octavius asked the Captain, "When does the Casino open."

"Shortly. We've probably passed the 12 mile limit already."

The Bear broke away for the moment and walked over to the table where Howard was seated. He leaned over and whispered, "After you've finished your meal, I'd like you to take a stroll through the casino. Watch and observe. Come back in time for the show at 8. Take an Ursula with you."

The porcupine nodded and said, "I might even place a bet or two."

Howard

The Great Bear chuckled. "Don't blame me if you lose all your quills. See you later. I have to do some more meet and greet. What a pain!"

Meanwhile, Belinda had been exploiting her showbear charm and posing for pictures with the VIPs. The females were looking lustfully at her jewelry. The males were looking lustfully at Belinda. Octavius returned. Between his size and net worth and her glamor and aristocracy, they were mesmerizing the diners. A number of feminine glances settled on the Great Bear.

The Elk and Captain were getting earfuls from the Old Faithfuls who were comparing the **SOLARWIND** to other Solar Seas ships they cruised on. Most of the comments were favorable. A few of the recollections were fictitious, remembering services the company never offered or maybe prodding management to include them on future voyages.

Captain Lion said, "Bearoness and gentlebeasts, please enjoy your dinners and drinks. I hope they're to your liking. Then we can go and greet our passengers in the neighboring venues, if you don't mind."

Octavius did mind but said nothing. He didn't envy the Captain or his staff, especially with the corporate bigwigs breathing down their necks. He just wanted to nab this threat monger and settle back for a leisurely ocean trip. Oh well, the champagne was vintage.

Octavius and the Bearoness finished their excellent meals and tailed along with the Captain and CEO to the other two restaurants where they were hosting the high priced tourists. They waved at the Octavians in the Solar Seas room and proceeded to meet and greet the rest. The pestiferous heifer took the opportunity to complain to "management" about not being seated in the Gourmet Gardens. After all, this was their third cruise with Solar Seas. She threatened it could well be their last. She also didn't like her suite or her butler. The Captain promised to look into it. Her husband who was a maritime expert in his own mind had a series of operational suggestions to improve the performance of this "weird" vessel. The CEO half listened with his eyes fixed elsewhere.

The welcoming party moved on to Tropical Temptations, the third and final venue where a riotous songfest had broken out, no doubt promoted by the vintage champagne. Waves, paw and hoof shakes, selfies, and several choruses of "Sailing, Sailing. Over the Bounding Main" punctuated by calls for more bubbly. The greeting foursome escaped back to the Gourmet Gardens and regrouped.

Bel sighed. "I suppose you're going to get the perpetual complainer on every trip, Captain."

"Yes, Bearoness, oops, Belinda. There's always one who thinks they are not getting all the attention they deserve. We have two passengers who have been on every cruise with us since our inaugural voyage back in the '90's. The Shearings. Texas Sheep. Sweetest folks you'd ever want to meet. They're here in the Gourmet Gardens tonight. I'll have them introduced to you. Not at all like that big-mouth heifer who thinks she should own the ship and the staff after three trips. She sounds off every time she embarks. I'd like to toss her overboard."

"Who are they, exactly?"

"Well, the two of them seem quite rich. He's supposed to be an oil tycoon. But from what I can tell, they've made a lot of enemies back in Texas and on previous cruises here on our ships. Several of the VIP passengers have accused them of cheating at cards. Our room stewards believe she engages in shoplifting. When they go to the casino or shoppes we keep a very careful eye on them."

"They both try to cover their tracks by being as obnoxious as possible. She accused her stewardess of stealing. No such thing. Next time they try to book on Solar Seas ships, no suitable accommodation will be available."

"Thanks for the warning, Captain. I'll make sure our party keeps clear of them as much as we can. We already have enough spoiling our trip with these threats."

"I'm sorry about that. I don't like her but I hope the CFO is right and this is all just a hoax."

"Me, too!"

The Development of Civilization Volume 18
Part 4
The Tarot

From "An Introduction to Faunapology"

by Octavius Bear Ph.D.

Cartomancy is fortune-telling or divination using a special deck of Tarot cards. It arose in Paris during the 1780s, using the Tarot of Marseilles. Cartomancers tell us that the entire universe exists within a Tarot deck, with each card representing a person, place, or event. The 78-card Tarot deck has two distinct parts:

The Major Arcana cards, which speak of greater secrets, and the Minor Arcana cards, which involve lesser mysteries. The Major Arcana or trumps, consists of 22 cards without suits.

The Minor Arcana has 56 cards, divided into four suits of 14 each. Ten numbered cards and four court cards. The court cards are the King, Queen, Knight and Page/Jack. The traditional Tarot suits are swords, batons, coins and cups.

The Major Arcana cards represent monumental, groundbreaking influences. Each stands alone as a powerful message, representing life-changing motions that define the beginnings or ends of cycles.

The Minor Arcana cards, on the other hand, reflect everyday matters. They are broken up into four suits, each containing ten numbered cards and four court cards. The card's number reveals the stage of an event: The ace card represents the beginning, while the 10 symbolizes the end.

Similarly, the court cards shows our understanding of circumstances on an individual level, representing either personality types or actual people.

There are a variety of possible spreads. One card, three card, five card. One card is often good for a yes or no answer while a more complex five card spread can be much more informative. The position of the card, upright or reversed, indicates a different message.

Chapter Nine

The theater is packed with new friends.
And Giselle's Tarot act just transcends.
With Sir Otto's assist,
She's too good to resist
And they buy what the dog recommends.

The **SOLARWIND**'s Caribbean Theater was SRO for the Welcome Aboard show. Promptly at 8, a pert Freddi Fox in her role as Social Directress and mistress of ceremonies introduced the show and put in not too subtle plugs for the ship's services, offerings and events.

The Great Bear, Belinda, the Twins and I occupied front row seats. The Frau, Wyatt, and the Flying Tigers were also front and center around us. Lord David and Dancing Dan sat with Jaguar Jack DeLad. Howard had just returned from his casino jaunt but didn't meet with Octavius.

Freddi set about introducing the first of the acts. "Ladies and Gentlebeasts, Music, Music, Music!" The band struck up a lively overture.

The Solar Seas Revue Company dancers and singers twirled and tapped onstage in a compilation of Caribbean music and footwork. Wild applause! Then came the individual acts – a comedian walrus, followed by my client Bearnice Blanc singing Broadway show tunes. The house went wild. More songs and dances by the Revue team and another of my proteges, Bearyl Blanc held the audience in her paws doing her composite dramatic readings.

And then: Madame Giselle, Queen of the Tarot and Sir Otto The Magnificent. Mystery! Magic! and Madcap Mirth!

They had been hard at work all day getting their act together. Their first performance at Polar Paradise last month had been a smash. I expected no less on this ship and I was right. Back then, Chita had been at the castle helping to work out the kinks, enhance the show biz values and develop the chatter and patter of the new act. Ursula had worked out an Augmented Reality process with Giselle, doing instant searches on her Tarot clients and flashing comments on Giselle's AR contact lenses so she could make 'amazing' comments and predictions. Freddi had spared no efforts in creating an aura of mystery in the theater lighting, décor and sound effects. The house band had worked up a series of mystical musical intros and stings to support Otto's and Giselle's spectacular feats.

The house lights dimmed once again and a drum roll grew in volume and speed. Otto "zapped' onstage from nowhere and executed a series of backflips ending in a kneeling bow with arms spread as the brass exploded with an exciting fanfare. Ta-Da! Excited applause. "How did he do that? Where did he come from?" The Octavians knew. The tourists didn't.

"Ladies and Gentlebeasts," he shouted, "Welcome to the Caribbean Theatre's Mélange of Mystical Mysteries. I am obviously not Madame Giselle. *(Laughter)* As you may have concluded, I am Hairy Otter, known in some circles as Sir Otto the Magnificent. We're delighted you've chosen to join us this evening. We are prepared to awe you and entertain you."

He bowed again, adjusted his tail and straightened his red satin jacket. "Now, let me introduce the mysterious mistress of cartomancy, Madame Giselle, Queen of the Tarot."

MADAME GISELLE WOOF - SIR OTTO THE MAGNIFICENT

The band played an exotic oriental melody as Giselle made her entrance, bathed in a spotlight. Clad in a sparkling gold lamé robe with a small matching turban perched between her ears, she bowed to the audience's enthusiastic applause, nodded to Otto and proceeded to the elaborately decorated table and chairs positioned in the center of the stage. Once she was seated, Otto looked at her and asked, "Madame, are the spirits active tonight?"

"Mais Oui, Sir Otto. They are quite eager to help our friends reach new wisdom."

"Well, let's begin!"

"Will you fetch the cards for me, please?"

Suddenly a cascade of Tarot cards *(under Otto's telekinetic control)* tumbled out of the air and landed in a neat stack in front of the Bichon. (Ooohs and aaahs from the audience.)

She barked, "Very clever, Mon Ami. Shall I do a quick reading for you?"

"Of course, make a prediction."

"First you must cut and shuffle the cards."

The deck rose from the table, broke into two halves, shuffled itself and settled back on the surface, face down. *(Amazed laughter)*

He chortled, "There! So much easier to let them do it themselves. You know what a klutz I am."

"Indeed, let me take a moment to explain the Tarot deck for those in the audience who are not familiar with it." She gave a short tutorial and then waved Otto into the other chair.

"You have just returned from several journeys, am I correct?"

"Unfortunately, yes! I'm worn out."

"Let us see if the cards have anything to say about your next trip. As you know, the Tarot is also known as the Fool's Journey. I shall take 3 cards."

"Well, I'm certainly the Fool."

She flipped the top card. "Indeed, you are. Here is the Fool. Let us take the next card. Ah. The Chariot. Your journey begins. And now The third

68

Card The Wheel of Fortune. Are you ready to embark and bring fortune with you?"

He disappeared. *(zapped)* Murmurs throughout the audience. Suddenly a squeaky voice resonated from the back of the room. "Here I am, Madame. Journey's end. I have your first seeker ready to join you. Come with me, Miss."

He led a slender gazelle up to the stage. "Madame Giselle. This is Ms. Georgianna Gazelle. She seeks your guidance."

"Thank you, Otto. Please be seated, Ms. Gazelle. Have we ever met or do we have mutual acquaintances?"

"Er, No! This is my first cruise. I just arrived today. I just wandered in here to see the show. I don't know either of you."

"D'accord!" A message flashed across her contact lenses. Ursula 16 on the job. "She's a kindergarten teacher on vacation, by herself and looking for romance."

"Am I correct that you are here alone?"

"Yes! I'm on vacation."

"Away from all those disrupting cubs, pups, calves, foals and kittens."

"How did you know I'm a kindergarten teacher?"

"The spirits informed me. Now let us see what is in store for you."

She handed the deck to the deer who clumsily cut and shuffled the cards and gave them back.

Giselle peeled off and laid out three cards. She turned them over slowly and said, "I see an important change in your life. A pleasant change. You will find romance soon."

Georgianna gasped, clasped Giselle's paw, stood up and stepped backwards on the stage. Otto was on the side of the room with a male red deer in tow. Ursula flashed on Giselle's contact lenses. "Single, rich, titled, stockbroker, socially unskilled."

"Bon Soir, Monsieur or should I call you Milord?"

He reacted in amazement. "I don't use that term but yes, I'm a member of the aristocracy."

"Je m'excuse de mon erreur. Are you an MP?"

"Actually, Yes.

"What can the spirits help you with?"

"I don't know. I'd just like something new in my life."

"Perhaps, *someone* new?"

"Well, yes!"

"Let us see!" She handed him the deck which he skillfully shuffled and then cut.

Otto chuckled. "Had some experience with cards, eh?"

"A bit." He placed the deck face down and Giselle picked off the top three cards.

"It seems you have attracted the ladies. The Queen of Wands, the Queen of Swords and the Empress. All good signs of a blossoming relationship."

Otto leaned over and said. "May I introduce you two. Milord, meet Georgianna. Georgianna meet Milord." Laughter and applause as the two of them left the stage.

And so it went. Otto amazing the audience with his slapstick tricks. Giselle pretending annoyance at his antics and reading the Tarot cards for six or seven more clients including Gladys Vaquero, the haughty heifer from the Captain's table. She disposed of her by predicting a troubled voyage. It was inevitable given her personality. Gladys was annoyed. The rest of Giselle's querents were sent off on much more positive notes.

Finally, on Otto's signal the band started to play Giselle's exit music. She rose and bowed. "Mesdames and Messieurs. Merci Beaucoup. My associate and I are so pleased that you have joined us this evening. I hope you feel the spirits made our little offering entertaining and valuable. Please join us again. We perform four nights a week here and in the Tropics

Lounge. I can also be reached by appointment as well. Thank you again. Au Revoir. Say goodnight, Otto!"

He sent the Tarot deck flying into the air, executed several back flips and caught the cards in a stack before they fell to the floor.

A standing ovation as the two of them took several bows while the band played their exit music. As the room started to empty, the Octavians ran up to the stage. Hugs and paw shakes. The Twins mobbed her. Octavius and Belinda were all smiles. Giselle was shaking with excitement and nervousness.

She turned to me. "Maury! Was it all right?"

I laughed. "All right? You and your river otter buddy were just sensational. Welcome to cruise ship show-biz."

*****

As the crowd left the theater, Howard sidled over to Octavius. "I have news and you won't like it."

"Did you lose at the Blackjack tables?"

"No! I actually won a few dollars but I made a discovery that's going to make you quite unhappy."

"All right. I've been unhappy most of the day. Lay it on me."

"I spotted the Casino Manager. Fortunately, he didn't spot me."

"Howard, are you trying to drag this out and be irritating? What about the Casino Manager?

"It's your rotten half-brother, Agrippa!"

"Ohmigod! Are you sure?"

"You can't mistake him. Tall, light brown fur, phony British accent, limp and all. You need to get him off this ship. Or get him in the brig. Do you think he's involved with those threats?"

"I wouldn't put it past him. After his treacherous performance on Rhea with Otis, Priscilla and Admiral Tumult. *(See Book 12 The Nut Case)*

He continued "I need to talk to the Purser and Security Officer."

The Greyhound and Freddi were outside the theater taken up in conversation with several of the Old Faithfuls. Octavius signaled to her and she broke off her chat leaving the Fox to continue the socializing. She joined the Great Bear and me.

"Maury, your performers were just sensational. They'll be packing the shows. Thanks, Doctor Bear, for bringing them to us. They're like a great family."

"I'm afraid there's another member of my family on board that I don't think you want anything to do with. Your Casino Manager!"

"Albeart? I know he's a bear but are you related?"

"He's my step brother and his name is Agrippa, not Albeart. How did you come to hire him?"

"Although he's a Brit, he lives in Lauderdale and he answered an ad we placed when our original manager quit two weeks ago. None of the assistants were up to the job but his credentials were exactly what we wanted."

"For a blackjack or poker dealer, maybe but not a casino manager."

"He said he managed the casino on the SS Sunbrite. He had letters of recommendation from their skipper and purser."

"Did you talk to either of them?"

"No. I was just happy to find him and I believed the letters. I shouldn't have? He seemed to be the real thing. He certainly could talk casino talk.

"My step brother is a bear faced liar. I wouldn't trust him to give you the right time. I'm sure the letters were forged. Let's get him up to your office."

She said, "You realize if he's a phony, this also puts you in a rather compromising position with Solar Seas management and the Captain."

"You mean guilt by association? I'm perfectly happy to drop this whole mess back in the cruise line's lap. I'm ready to spend the next thirteen days relaxing in my suite, the restaurants or on the VIP pool deck with a drink in my paw. I found a bar that stocks mead, if you can believe it. We are getting involved to help you, the Captain and your Security Officer out. I don't need any suspicious glares from your sourpuss CFO or anyone else from Solar Seas front offices. Agrippa is a liar and a cheat and you need to get rid of him before he does some serious damage."

"Do you think he's behind those threats?"

"I don't know but I wouldn't put it past him. Let's summon him."

"OK, my office."

They trudged off, gathering the troops as they went.

The Purser shook her head. "One more problem I don't need. She keyed her radio. Commander Diomede to the Purser's office, please. ASAP.

The Security Officer responded. 'On my way. Is backup required?"

She looked at Octavius who shook his head negatively. "We can handle him."

Chapter Ten

Who's the Bear on the front of this book?
It's Agrippa – a liar and crook!
He's a grifter. Self-taught!
While he often is caught,
He just cleverly gets off the hook

Agrippa - The Bear Faced Liar

Crowded into Commander Gillian Greyhound's office, the Purser, Security Officer Diomede, Chief Engineer Pronghorn, Octavius, Bel, Howard, Otto, Ursula and I waited for "Albeart" Agrippa to make an appearance. A knock on the door. A snuffling sound,

The Purser called, "Come in, Albeart." As the door pushed open, she added "or should I say, Agrippa."

The bear limped in, looked around the room and snorted, "You summoned me, Commander. A problem? We just opened. Who are all these animals? I say, who is this Agrippa you mentioned?"

Octavius snorted back. "You, step-brother. Cut the innocent act! Howard, Belinda, Otto, Maury and I all recognize you and know you never managed a casino in your entire life. You're a poker dealing sharpie!"

"Lie, lies! I'm a victim of malicious slander. In my extensive past history, I have dealt games of chance for a living but always honestly. That's the truth."

"You wouldn't know the truth if it bit you. There are 17 Octavians on this ship, most of whom know you. Do you want me to bring them in and have them identify you and recall your gambling history? Should I get Juno, our mother, on the videophone. She'd love to hang you. "

He looked around. "Oh, all right. I lied on my credentials. This opportunity was just too good to pass up. Casino Manager on the newest cruise ship afloat with all the ergonomic bells and whistles. Loads of gamblers. You caught me. What are you going to do?"

The Purser replied. "That depends on you. First off, you're fired. I can't have an unqualified, dishonest and deceitful animal running our casino. The Cruise Lines International Association would have our necks. To make matters worse, our corporate officers are on board. They'll demand to know why I hired you. My job is in jeopardy thanks to you."

Security Officer Diomede stared at him. "Now, what to do about your lying and fraudulent credentials? I can slap you in our brig and turn you over to the authorities when we get back to Lauderdale or you can tell us about the threats we've been receiving and maybe we can be more lenient."

"What threats?"

Octavius laughed. "This ship has been receiving menacing emails. You either are the originator of them or you know who is."

"I just landed a cushy job running the table games and slots on a ship that's soon to become famous. I'd have to be crazy to try and ruin that."

"But you know who is behind them, don't you?"

A long pause. "All right! Yes, I do. But it's not me. He's blackmailing me. Either I keep quiet or he tells management I'm a fraud. He's planning to hit this ship with ransomware."

"Who is it?"

"It's Otto's old friend. Mattingly Owl."

Mattingly Owl was a freelance cyber mercenary. (*See Book 15 A Case for the Birds*) Octavius had often wondered where he was hanging out nowadays. "Is he still employed by General Turmoil?"

"No, He's hired out to the Mystical Mardi Gras Cruise Line in New Orleans. They're launching a new program with repurchased luxury ships that still use Heavy Fuel Oil. They want to ruin **SOLARWIND's** reputation for ecology."

Mattingly Owl

Engineer Pruitt Pronghorn suddenly looked up. "Has it been you who's been diddling with our elevators?"

"No, it's Mattingly. He's been testing out his remote malware systems. Just like he did on Rhea. Remember, Otto?"

The Otter squeaked, "Boy, do I. He's not on this ship?"

"Of course not. He'll be hundreds of miles away, maybe thousands."

"Octavius grunted, "When is he going to attack?"

"I don't know, Certainly while the reporters and Solar Seas bigwigs are still on board. Maximum embarrassment!"

The Great Bear turned to the Purser, "When are the press and management scheduled to leave?"

"When we reach San Juan. In five days!"

"All right. We reach two ports before that. Nassau and St. Thomas. He'll probably attack on a sea day. We have some work to do. Engineer Pronghorn, can you gather your techies? We need a complete inventory of the ship's technical vulnerabilities. We'll give your staff protective instructions. "

"Howard, Otto, we need to get going. Contact Condo. Get them ready for some cyberwarfare. Prep the Ursulas. We'll be docking soon at Nassau. I hope Chita's there. Maury, charter a plane. We're flying Madame Catt to New Orleans. We'll beard Mystical Mardi Gras in its den…or dock. Agrippa, we are going out on a limb on your say so. If you're not telling the truth, this ship's brig will only be the beginning of your problems."

"Octavius, I am wounded. This ship is in trouble. Mattingly is getting his ransomware ready and Mardi Gras is paying the bill. Those are the facts. Would I lie?"

The Great Bear and the assembled Octavians roared with laughter.

The Development of Civilization Volume 18
Part 5
<u>Malware and Ransomware</u>
From "An Introduction to Faunapology"

by Octavius Bear Ph.D.

<u>Malware</u>, or "malicious software," describes any malevolent program or code that is intentionally harmful to systems. Hostile, intrusive, and intentionally vicious, malware seeks to invade, damage, or disable computers, computer systems, computer supported equipment, networks, tablets, and mobile devices, often by taking partial control over a device's operations. It may also leak private information, gain unauthorized access to information or systems, deprive users access to information or interfere with the user's computer security and privacy. Don't confuse it with a software bug that causes harm due to some error or deficiency.

The defense strategies against malware differ according to the type of attack but most can be thwarted by installing antivirus software, creating firewalls, applying regular security patches , securing networks, having regular backups and isolating infected systems.

<u>Ransomware</u> is a type of malware that threatens to perpetually block access to data and systems unless a ransom is paid. While some simple ransomware may lock the system without damaging any files, more advanced malware uses a technique called cryptoviral extortion. It encrypts the victim's files, making them inaccessible, and demands a ransom payment to decrypt them. In a properly implemented cryptoviral extortion attack, recovering the files without the decryption key is an intractable problem and making tracing and prosecuting the perpetrators difficult.

Ransomware prevents a user from accessing their files until a ransom is paid. There are two variations of ransomware, being crypto ransomware and locker ransomware. Locker ransomware just locks down a computer system without encrypting its contents, whereas crypto ransomware locks down a system and encrypts its contents.

Once malicious software is installed on a system, it is essential that it stays concealed, to avoid detection. Software packages known as rootkits allow this concealment, by modifying the host's operating system so that the malware is hidden from the user. Rootkits can prevent a harmful process from being visible in the system's list of processes or keep its files from being read.

In some cases, a direct monetary ransom may not be demanded if the intent is to simply create severe damage. This may be the case with SOLARWIND. Envision a tropical cruise ship without power, controls, light, air conditioning or facilities having to be towed into the nearest port to unload over a thousand enraged passengers and reporters onto an unprepared terminal and port. Imagine having to reset the ship's entire technology before it can move again on its own power. Or having to submit the vessel for salvage. The financial, reputational and regulatory impact on Solar Seas Company may be irreparable, possibly leading to bankruptcy.

Can ransomware be prevented or defeated? In proper circumstances, yes. The UUI Advanced Super Computing Center at the Deep Data Hexagon back in Kentucky has a specialty team devoted to this kind of cyber warfare. We will summon them into action. Mattingly is skilled but he's not unbeatable.

There are a number of tools intended specifically to decrypt files and programs locked by ransomware, although successful recovery may not always be possible. Time and our efforts will tell.

Chapter Eleven

Say Hello to the stylish Ms. Catt.
Or just Chita whenever you chat.
Independent and smart.
Trouble shooting's her art.
She is always right where danger's at.

Chita

A small crowd gathered at the Nassau Cruise Ship Terminal-Festival Place to see the unusual ship arrive. Once again the news media were active with helicopters, speed boats and drones all recording the event. A small 'meet and greet' delegation including a local calypso band was on hand. Bursts of sound from the ship's horn merged with the thumps of the steel drums. Tourists both on and off the vessel clapped their hands and laughed uproariously.

As the **SOLARWIND** docked at its mooring, a taxi from Nassau International Airport dropped off a sultry spotted cat wearing her trademark diamond collar. Chita had arrived and proceeded with her baggage cart past the shoppes and exhibits, out through the gates and on to the slip where the ship will unload its crowd of passengers eager for a day at the port and the island.

Waiting for the gangways to lower, she stared up at the VIP portal, spied Otto and me and waved. We waved back, Little does she know.

The mob of passengers, unaware of the possible difficulties they may encounter back on the **SOLARWIND**, debark for a day at Nassau or leave for a longer stay at Paradise Island at the fabulous Atlantis resort. They swoop down the passageways, checking out with the guards as they go while Otto and I are negotiating with Security Officer Diomede to allow Madame Catt to board.

As the crowd thinned, she strutted up the gangway and high fived Otto and me. Freddi Fox is there to greet her as part of the Octavian entourage.

"Hello, Madame Catt! May I call you Chita? Welcome aboard the **SOLARWIND.** We have you in a suite on the Empire Deck above the bridge. A separate bedroom and bath sharing the common area with the Flying Tigers. Here is your keycard. Come with me and I'll introduce you to Sylvester, your butler."

Otto looked at the cat. "Don't unpack. Unfortunately, Octavius has an assignment for you and Jack in New Orleans. We've chartered a jet for you."

"New Orleans? I only left there a few days ago. When Maury called, I was looking forward to a little Caribbean R&R even though I hate water."

"Well, this won't take long. We'll pick you up again day after tomorrow in St. Thomas at the airport and transfer you back to the ship at Havensight Dock. Meanwhile, Octavius wants to see you ASAP."

"So do I. To give him a piece of my mind."

On to the Empire Deck and her shared suite. Say hello to Sylvester, the butler. The Tiger Twins were off on a shore trip. Then on to the Imperial Suite, temporary sea home of Octavius and Belinda, where we were greeted by their butler, Carlos.

"I'm Chita! Where's Octavius?"

"Right this way, Madame and Gentlebeasts. Doctor Bear and the Bearoness are in the lounge."

Freddi said her good-byes and left Otto and me to listen to Ms. Catt have her hissy fit.

"Octavius! You interrupt my work for UUI in London, get me on a long distance flight to Nassau and now Otto tells me you want me to go back to New Orleans. I was just there and didn't care very much for it. What is this? Are you just trying to jerk me around?"

"No, my dear cat. I'm sorry for the run around but there's a critical mission I need you to perform. It won't take long but I want you and Jaguar Jack to apply a bit of pressure on the Ocelot who's president and CEO of Mystical Mardi Gras Cruise Line in New Orleans. Felines to feline! His name is Oscar Ocelot and he's hired Mattingly Owl to cyberattack and cripple this ship. They want to ruin its maiden voyage and severely damage the Solar Seas Company. We want you two heavyweights to get them to call the Owl off."

"The same Mattingly Owl of exoplanet Rhea and General Turmoil fame?"

"Got it in one! We don't know where he is or when he's scheduled to strike but we do know who he's working for. We know all this from Agrippa who lied his way into managing the casino on board the **SOLARWIND**. We have Condo, Byzz, and some of the Ursulas standing by back at the Hex to counter attack if necessary. You will be our messengers. 'Back Mattingly off or else Mardi Gras will have a useless fleet.'"

"How does Agrippa figure in all this?"

The Great Bear explained his step brother's lies, treachery, confession and activities leading up to the potential crisis.

"But you believe him now?"

"His tail's in the wringer."

"All the more reason to doubt him. Never did like Agrippa. As I remember, neither do you or your mother. Is he still on the ship?"

"Yes! In the brig!"

"Good! OK. Off to the Big Easy! Is Jaguar Jack read in?"

"He's been briefed and is waiting for you. We've chartered a high speed bizjet for your trip. Maury is coming with you but he won't make the actual call on Mystical Mardi Gras. We want two formidable cats to deliver our counter threat. Maury and Ursula will fill you in further on your flight."

"All right! A quick lunch and we're on our way. Hello Belinda! Good bye Belinda! Nice to have seen you again, Belinda. Ha!"

"You too, Chita. Hurry back. There are a lot of fun things to do on this ship including shop for expensive jewelry. The shoppes are closed now.

"It's a date! And you're paying, Octavius! So long! Hey Carlos, where can a cat get something to eat on this sea-going mansion? Weird looking ship. What's with those crazy masts?"

"Come with me, Senora Catt. There's a nice sea food restaurant that's open for the stay-on-board VIP guests. Wonderful fish! I think you'll like it. Those masts are windsails and solar panels. We get most of our power from the sun and the breezes. Very ergonomic. That's why she's called the **SS SOLARWIND** and the company is Solar Seas. Doctor Bear and Bearoness, I shall be right back. Do you need anything before I leave?"

"Only the answers to a few hundred questions, Carlos."

The butler laughed, confused as usual by the cryptic comments of the Great Bear. He thought to himself. "What a crazy bunch! Oh well, He'll probably be a good tipper. I hope so."

Off they went.

Chapter Twelve

Our Belinda meets Harriet Hare
For an interview in a deck chair.
The reporter makes note
Of why Bel's on the boat
With the Twins, such a rascally pair.

"Bel, I'm on my way to brief the Captain, Purser, Chief Security Officer Diomede and Chief Engineer Pronghorn on our plan. I'll have to inform Wally Wapiti, CEO of Solar Seas as well as his COO, Coleman Cougar and Corporate Security Officer Pablo Puma. He may bring along Bill Beaver, the marketeer; Corporate Attorney Emilia Emu and our highly unenthusiastic critic, CFO Loretta Lynx. I'll ask her to spring for Maury's, Jack's and Chita's trip and her new jewelry. That should be a laugh."

"They're aware of Mystic Mardi Gras' opposition to the **SOLARWIND** but they may not know they've hired the Owl to cripple this ship with all the VIPs and reporters on board."

"OK, Tavi. I'm heading down to the VIP pool deck. With most of the passengers gone ashore, maybe I can get in a good solo swim. The Twins have also elected to stay on board. Strange! I would have thought they'd want to go sightseeing in Nassau. Maybe they're plotting out their next game- *Bears at Sea.* Anyhow, let me know how things go with the Solar Seas officials."

*****

There were a few VIP diehards who chose to remain on board the ship. Some had done Nassau and Paradise Island before and some like Belinda wanted to take advantage of the absence of crowds even though the VIP decks were always sparsely populated. A couple of animals lined poolside and a few basked on lounge chairs. And then there was...

..."Hi Mom! Watch me, a Kodiak Polar cannonball!" Splash!

"Oooh McTavish. I don't need any help getting wet but now that you set it off, I'll do a few laps. This isn't the biggest swim venue in the world but I can still get some exercise. I wish I could get your father to go swimming. He almost did in Australia. Mmm! This water's too warm. Not cold like Polar Paradise. Maybe we should have gone on an Arctic cruise."

After traversing the pool a dozen times, she hauled herself up over the edge, shook her fur, stood and went in search of some towels. She smiled at her neighbors after finding the towel locker, returned and settled onto a lounge, adjusting her sunglasses. A pair of shadows fell on her. The Social Directress and an unidentified female hare."

Freddi Fox said, "Good morning Bearoness. I hope I'm not disturbing you or your children but I wanted to introduce you to Harriet Hare. She writes a column for tourist industry magazines, news sheets and websites. "*Cruise Debuts*." She also does podcasts and a community forum on the latest developments in cruising. Needless to say, she's very interested in **SOLARWIND** and all of its ecological innovations."

The Hare twitched her nose and ears simultaneously, giggled and said, "Hello, Bearoness Belinda. I'm not just interested in the ship. I'm also interested in her famous and well-to-do passengers. And that certainly describes you and your husband. Your Twins are also well known for their electronic games. I understand you also have many of Doctor Bear's and your own associates along with you. The Octobers?"

Belinda laughed. "No, the Octavians. Yes, we've just about filled up the Empire deck."

Harriet held up a portable recorder and cell phone camera. "I wonder if I could impose on you to grant me a brief interview. I'll make it as painless as possible. I don't suppose Doctor Bear might also be available."

"No, he's not. He's taken up with business. We're both semi-retired but you wouldn't believe it to watch us. He still runs Universal Ursine Industries and I own a substantial castle/resort in The Shetlands. Maybe you'd like to give that a mention. It's called Polar

Paradise. We're thinking of building a cruise ship dock there. Nothing settled yet.

Freddi Fox looked at the Bearoness hopefully. Belinda chuckled to herself. "The price of fame and fortune. It's not as if I haven't been interviewed before. Wealthy star of The Aquabears and Pavel Polar's movies, Scots nobility, resort proprietor. Married to a giga billionaire tycoon, scientist and criminologist. Mother of the fabulous game creating Twins. Oh well. Freddi looks so eager. OK, let's talk! If it helps the ship and its crew. They could use some good publicity. Maybe more if that lousy Owl pulls off his attack. Way to go, Agrippa! You creep!"

She looked at the fox and the reporter. "OK, let's chat but on one condition."

"Yes?"

"You're both standing in the sun. Please move!"

Another round of giggles. This time from both of them.

She looked into the pool where the Twins were cavorting. "Kids, come on out and be interviewed. This lady is doing a feature on us. You can plug your latest game – *Bears at Sea.*

Splash! The two hybrid bears swam across, jumped up on the wall of the pool, grabbed towels and ran over to Belinda's lounge chair. They looked at Freddi whom they recognized and gave her a big 'Hello'. "Hi, Commander Fox. Any good games on tap for today?"

"Yes, we have a couple of Trivial Pursuit contests after lunch today, *(The twins always cheated. They used Ursula.)* plus a multi-deck Scavenger Hunt planned for tomorrow night as we leave St. Thomas after most of the passengers have returned from their port day."

Arabella clapped her paws and said, "I love Scavenger Hunts. We win a lot of them. I once brought back a dinosaur bone."

"Sorry, no dinosaurs on a cruise ship."

McTavish laughed. "What about a whale? We know a couple."

"Afraid not!"

"Well, we'll win anyway!"

The Social Directress said, "Excuse me. There's a lecture I have to organize right now." She walked off. The Twins turned to the columnist. "Hi! We're McTavish and Arabella Bear. Octavius Bear is our father and the Bearoness here is our Mom. They're very smart and so are we. Do you know about our internet games – *The Bold Brave Brilliant Bumptious Bears* and *Bears in Space?* We're working on a new one - *Bears at Sea.* It features the **SOLARWIND,** its crew, the Octavians and of course, the two of us.

Bel took a swipe at them. "OK, you've made your pitch. Now, calm down and let Ms. Hare ask her questions."

"Sure, fire away, Harriet!"

"Wonderful! I have a few things my readers, watchers and listeners want to know. Let me turn on my recorder and camera."

Belinda and Arabella primped. McTavish flopped on a lounge chair.

Showtime!

"Bearoness! What brings you and your companions to the luxury decks of the **SOLARWIND**?" The travel columnist aimed her camera and recorder at Belinda.

"Well, Harriet, as you know my husband, Doctor Octavius Bear, is the famous scientist, criminologist, charitable contributor and giga-millionaire owner of worldwide Universal Ursine Industries. I am a member of Scots nobility, the former leading lady of the Aquabear Revue - *Some Like it Cold* - the current owner of the Polar Paradise castle/resort in the Shetlands and actress in Pavel Polar's adventure films. We are both semi-retired and are taking time to travel and enjoy the Earth and several exoplanets with our children and associates. We recently spent time in Australia and have had some interesting off-planet experiences. We decided to sail on this ecologically responsible vessel to show our support for non-polluting cruising and of course, to visit the wonders of the Caribbean."

"You two are perfect examples of the enlightened global rich and famous. I'm sure my readers and watchers are familiar with all of the splendid causes you fund."

"I doubt if they know about all of them. Some are confidential but yes, we want our money to be used for good. We are most fortunate to have it and we want the world to take advantage of it. I would be lying if I said I do not enjoy a bit of indulgences such as this ship affords but we like to combine luxury with social benefits. If **SOLARWIND** is a success, it will mean a dramatic change in cruising and cruise ship development. Our team is paying full price for our travel and contributing extra to support the Solar Seas Company's efforts."

"Tell me about your team! The Octavians."

"They're a diverse bunch! They come from all over the world and represent many of the world's major species - feline, canine, suricate, rodent, lutrine, dolphins, primates, condors and of course, ursines. They are a highly experienced group, each with special talents."

"I caught the Welcome Aboard show last night. The entertainers in your group are fabulous."

"Yes, they are but each one of them is also a skilled crime fighter. Sir Otto was recently knighted by an exoplanet emperor for rescuing his daughter and Madame Giselle helped put a drug lord out of business permanently.

"Oh, how exciting. I have to talk with them."

"You can catch them after tomorrow night's show, The theater is dark on port days.

"Speaking of talents, your Twin offspring are quite remarkable."

McTavish and Arabella, wonder of wonders, had been standing by quietly listening to this conversation. That came to an end.

As the camera and recorder turned their way, Arabella blurted. "Right, Miss Hare. We're unusual hybrids. Our parents, a Kodiak and a Polar bear can breed but they seldom do. We look different. Half brown and half white. Our noses, ears and tails are unusual. Our parents are super-smart and so are we.

Belinda raised a paw. "You also have a distinct lack of modesty."

McTavish interrupted. "Well, we are highly intelligent, Mom. You and Dad know that. Didn't we pick this ship for our cruise? Us and Ursula."

Your grammar's terrible!

"Gramma Juno? No, she's not, She's great!"

Harriet chuckled and asked, "Who's Ursula?"

Before the Twins could answer, Belinda said, "She's a friend."

McTavish continued, "Our internet games are world renowned. We have thousands of fans around the globe. Even Australia."

Arabella said, "We've been lots of places and met lots of folks. Including lots of bad guys."

Her brother said, "Yeah, speaking of bad guys. We have a step uncle, Agrippa. Dad and Gramma Juno can't stand him. He ran this ship's casino for a short while but he's a liar and a crook and he's locked in the brig until we get back to Fort Lauderdale."

Arabella smiled at the columnist. "Isn't that exciting? We're going to put that in our next game - *Bears at Sea!*"

Belinda winced and said "I think that ends our interview. I look forward to seeing your column and podcast. Thank you, Harriet."

"Thank you, Bearoness. Oh dear, my next appointment is with the Vaqueros. He's such a blowhard and she's a royal pain. I think I'll interview them and manage to lose the material. Maybe not! She'd manage to blow a gasket. What a pest! Not at all like the Shearings. Two of the loveliest sheep you'd ever want to meet. You really should meet them. Ask Freddi to introduce you."

Chapter Thirteen

The Great Bear gets some grief from the Lynx.
But the Frau lets her know what she thinks.
She sticks up for her Boss.
Says Agrippa's a loss.
And her snide attitude really stinks.

Meanwhile, Octavius, the Frau, Colonel Where, Otto and Howard trooped into the bridge conference room to give a situation report to the ship's chain of command and the management of Solar Seas. Before they could all be seated, the CFO, Loretta Lynx sniffed, snarled and snapped. "Well, *Mister* Bear, what have you got us wasting our money on now? I wouldn't be surprised if you and your minions were responsible for those amateurish threats. Is it true your brother is running our casino under false pretenses?"

Before Octavius could say anything, Frau Schuylkill rumbled a threatening growl. "No, madam, we are not responsible for those messages. We resent your accusations. And as for Agrippa Bear. He is currently in the ship's brig awaiting arrest for fraud when we return to Fort Lauderdale. He is Doctor Bear's half brother and has been a thorn in all of our sides for many years. He is a bear faced liar. Now, do you want to hear of our plans to counteract Mystical Mardi Gras' plot or are you too influenced by your own stupid prejudices to listen."

Frau Schuylkill

90

The Lynx was dumbstruck but recovered enough to begin a reply. The CEO, Wally Wapiti, shook his heavily antlered head and said, "Shut up, Loretta. I believe and trust these folks." The rest of the managers and the ship's commanders nodded in agreement. "Go ahead, _Doctor_ Bear."

Octavius gently smiled. "Thank you President Wapiti. And thanks to the rest of your team and the **SOLARWIND's** commanders for your confidence. As you know, this was to be a leisurely holiday for my wife, kids and me as well as my Octavian team. It's turning out to be anything but. I'd rather be relaxing on the balcony of my suite but for the moment, it's not to be"

"It seems this ship may be a source of aggravation to other companies in the industry. According to our sources, Mystical Mardi Gras decided to do something about it. We believe they hired the services of a highly skilled but morally deficient technology expert named Mattingly Owl to wage a cyberattack against **SOLARWIND.** We've worked both with him and against him in the past. This time we're in major opposition. His plan is to totally cripple the ship's electronics with all of the VIPs and reporters still on board. Major disruption. Terrible publicity, disgruntled tourists, worldwide political and financial issues."

"Madam Lynx, Mr. Cougar, Mr. Beaver, Ms. Emu, Mr. Wapiti, Captain Lion - Imagine a tropical cruise ship like **SOLARWIND** dead in the water. No power, controls, lights, air conditioning, communications, elevators, kitchens, sick bay or other facilities. Needing to be towed into the nearest port to unload over a thousand outraged passengers and reporters. Imagine the local harbor authorities and government hit with an unprepared terminal and insufficient housing to accommodate the evacuees. Imagine having to reconstruct the ship's entire computer and propulsion technology before it can move on its own power. Or, worse yet, submitting the vessel for salvage. The operational, financial, marketing and regulatory impact on Solar Seas Company may be irreparable, possibly leading to bankruptcy."

The expressions of horror on the faces of his audience said it all.

"Can ransomware be prevented or defeated? In many cases, yes. Our UUI Advanced Super Computing Center back in Kentucky has a specialty team devoted to this kind of cyber warfare. If necessary, we will call them into action. Mattingly is skilled but he's not unbeatable. We're sending a delegation to New Orleans right now to persuade, nay, threaten Mardi Gras. If they allow the Owl to persist, we will say we're ready to injure their entire fleet of current and newly acquired ships. It's probably illegal but I don't believe threat of a lawsuit on our part will be sufficiently persuasive."

The group reluctantly agreed. The lawyer, however, reacted. "Doctor Bear, if indeed this Owl does attack the **SOLARWIND** and we retaliate, not only will we have to deal with our own wounded vessel and all the other impacts you've outlined, we will no doubt also be up to our collective ears in suits and countersuits and probable criminal prosecution for damaging Mardi Gras. I can't allow that to happen."

Octavius nodded. "I agree, Ms. Emu. I am counting on the threat of retaliation to get Mardi Gras to shut Mattingly down. My staff people who are on their way to New Orleans can be quite persuasive. We can also use a small demonstration to help things along. A minor disruption such as this ship suffered with its elevators."

The Chief Engineer cursed under his breath. "So you think those glitches came from this Owl."

"Our experts are rather confident that they did."

The Elk looked at the Engineer. "What glitches?"

"Before you came on board, sir, we were experiencing intermittent failures in the elevator control systems. We did a clean boot on the software and installed a fresh and updated version of the programs. There's been no further problem. But you think, Doctor Bear, that we were attacked."

'We think the Owl was experimenting and testing. We're not sure what's next."

The Lynx screamed "Well don't just sit there, you big oaf. Do something."

Chapter Fourteen

Is the Mardi Gras line such a threat?
There's no evidence of it as yet.
To fob off his misdeed
Did Agrippa mislead?
If he did he will soon feel regret.

As the Embraer Legacy 600 bizjet swiftly rose from the runway at Nassau International Airport and headed northwest over the Atlantic, the southern tip of Florida and the Gulf of Mexico to New Orleans, the two big cats, small Maury *(me)* and the ubiquitous Ursula plotted out their 'visit' to Oscar Ocelot - president and CEO of Mystical Mardi Gras Cruise Line.

Jaguar Jack pondered, "Maury, assuming he'll talk to us at all, he's obviously going to deny any involvement with a cyberattack or even knowing Mattingly Owl. What's our story? Once he knows why we're there, he'll probably toss us out."

I smiled, "I'm sure Mystical Mardi Gras is not in the best economic shape to acquire those refurbished ships. That's why I set up the meeting to discuss an unidentified tycoon's interest in investing in a mid-size cruise line. Under no circumstances do we identify Octavius. We *(you)* are the advance party, exploring the possibilities with different companies. Cats to cats!"

Ursula rang her chime and said, "In the conversation, you should slip in the investor's concern about pollution issues with HFO fueled cruise vessels and mention the **SOLARWIND** and The Solar Seas Company as being of interest to him. Let's see what the Ocelot says and take it from there. We need to deliver our own threat. Don't mention the Hex but ensure he knows we also have strong malware and ransomware attack and defense abilities. You're dangerous."

The two cats snarled and broke into gales of laughter.

I laughed too. "Got it? Great! Meanwhile, how about a few bizjet snacks?"

"And a bowl of champagne!" said Chita.

*****

New Orleans. Touchdown at MSY Airport and on to a hotel near the NOLA cruise ship piers and the offices of the Mystical Mardi Gras Cruise Lines. Chita and Jack were both up for a spicy creole meal and some hot jazz. Me too. Our appointment was for 10 tomorrow. Here we come, Oscar!

Next morning: The Jaguar burped. "Oof, that fish jambalaya was something else. How do you handle that, Chita?"

"You forget I was here for a couple of weeks while we took on the drug lord, Gaston. I got plenty of opportunity to soak up New Orleans cooking. The spicier the better. What about you, Maury?"

"For me, a little goes a long way. We'll have another chance later today for lunch, dinner and more music before we fly to St. Thomas tomorrow morning. Are you ready to see the Mystical Mardi Gras Maven? I'll meet you in an hour back at the building's entrance."

Off they went.

The cruise line's offices were on top of the Julia Street Cruise Terminal. More efficient than opulent, the executive floor windows had a wide view of the water. At the moment a ship was docked at the pier opposite. It was not one of Mardi Gras'.

At a desk crowded with phones, computer screens, two keyboards and *(electronic)* mice, a gold nameplate identified Roberta Bobcat, a female feline secretary. She sat in front of a central glassed-in office. No doubt, the CEO's. There were six offices in all. Functional fluorescent lighting illuminated the area. Several other animals sat at similar desks that took up most of the remaining floor space. Shredders, printers and file cabinets surrounded the desks. Color pictures of cruise ships and tropical ports of call lined the walls. A large model of a Mardi Gras Cruiser sat in the center of the room. *The Tropical Breeze*.

Jaguar Jack, carrying an Ursula laptop, approached the desk and said, "Mr. Jacques and Ms. Katrin to see Mr. Ocelot. We have an appointment." He extended their phony business cards.

The secretary gave them what looked like a smile and said, "Of course! Mr. Ocelot will be with you in a moment. May I get you something to drink?"

Jack was about to accept but Chita cut him off. "Thank you. It's not necessary."

The PA rose from her table, knocked on the office door and walked in gesturing for them to follow. A small spotted wildcat came out from behind his desk, looked up at the taller felines and smiled. He examined their business cards. "Thank you Bobbi.' She left. "Mr. Jacques and Ms. Katrin. Facilitators. Welcome to Mystical Mardi Gras Cruise Lines. I assume you are not here to book passage." A feral grin. "Please sit down. Let's get right to it. Your message said you represented a wealthy and mysterious client who might be interested in investing in a cruise line. Correct?"

Jacques (Jack) cleared his throat. It came out as a minor roar. Katrin (Chita) chirped and said. "Correct. Let's just say we are on a preliminary exploratory mission. Our wealthy investor is unsure whether he wants to get involved in the tourist business. Of course, there are other leisure options besides cruise lines and there are other lines besides Mystical Mardi Gras."

The Ocelot shook his head. "All true. What led you to our organization?"

Jack's turn. He had laid his laptop on the CEO's desk. Ursula was passively recording the conversation plus making silent observations of her own. The Jaguar replied. "Your cruise line is a medium size operation which would fit into his venture capital range. Though, perhaps you are no longer medium. We have been given to understand that you are considering expanding and acquiring several refurbished ships from one of the larger companies."

"This industry is awash with rumors. Our expansion plans, if any, are very much at the formative and confidential stage. New ships? He shrugged. Do you realize the costs involved in building a new cruise ship or even bringing one up to date? The tourism market is at a low ebb and revenue has all but disappeared. But the operating expenses don't go away. Every company is looking for ways to cut costs. Reducing staff and selling off vessels are two major alternatives."

He continued, "Forgive me, but your credentials are a bit hazy. I really don't know who you or your 'client' are. You could be the press or represent a competitor doing intelligence gathering."

Chita replied, "Yes, we could but we're not. We are actually researching several companies for different clients. For example, I assume you are aware of Solar Seas and its new ecology friendly ship – *SOLARWIND*."

"Now there is one of the bright spots on an otherwise gloomy cruise horizon. I want that ship. New! Innovative! Exciting! Popular! Efficient! Compliant! If you represent someone who is willing to try to acquire *SOLARWIND,* I'm interested in meeting with him or her."

"You don't see the ship as a threat?"

"Hell, no. I see it as the future."

Chita stared. "Interesting! Well, thanks for your time, Mr. Ocelot. We'll talk to our client. We may be back to you on a confidential non-disclosure basis."

The spotted cat frowned, "I still don't know who you guys are or who you represent."

"Sorry! You have your secrets. We have ours. Thanks for meeting with us."

They rose, took up the laptop and left the office. The Ocelot followed them out and scratched his head. "Bobbi! I think those two were imposters. What do we know about them?"

"Only what they told us, Mr. Ocelot. A phone call setting up an appointment *(Ursula)* and their business cards."

"Let me know immediately if either of them calls again. That meeting was very strange."

*****

Chita and Jack met Maury at the building entrance.

"How did it go? Is he the guy paying Mattingly?"

Chita growled, "Either he's a hell of a liar or we're barking up the wrong tree. He's a **SOLARWIND** enthusiast! Damaging the ship and its reputation is the last thing he wants. In fact, he wants the ship, himself. What do you think, Ursula?"

"I just did a further check on him with the Deep Data mavens, Chita. He seems to be an honest cruise industry enthusiast. I doubt he's our culprit."

Jack snarled, "Maury, let's blow off New Orleans and get down to St. Thomas ASAP. We should huddle with Octavius as soon as **SOLARWIND** reaches port. I think we also want to have a meaningful discussion with Agrippa. Why is he painting Mystic Mardi Gras as the bad guys? A little misdirection?"

The Cheetah chirped. "I wouldn't put it past him. He's not doing this on his own, though. He's not that smart and he hasn't got the resources. Someone else is steering him. Someone with clout. Let's get out of here, Maury. Suddenly, I've had enough of the Big Easy."

"OK!' I replied, "Let's check out of the hotel. Ursula, call Octavius and then call the airport and the pilots. We're leaving a day early. We'll get to St. Thomas before the ship arrives. The three of you can brief me fully as we travel. This whole thing smells funny."

Jack laughed. "No, amigo. It reeks."

Chapter Fifteen

What to say about Mattingly Owl?
He is clearly a treacherous fowl.
In his clandestine nest,
He is trying his best
To send ransomware out on the prowl.

Ursula relayed the results of the big cats' meeting with the Ocelot to Octavius. He was upset and puzzled. His step-brother had scored again. Lies! But why? No money has been demanded. Agrippa didn't stand to gain from a disaster on the ship. Or maybe he did. Had someone paid him off to mislead Solar Seas management, the ship's commanders and the Octavians about Mystical Mardi Gras? That ship line didn't seem to be involved.

What about Mattingly himself? Did he send the threats? Was the Owl working alone? Was he engaging in technological extortion? If so, why? Was he actually planning an attack? Was he going to do anything at all? Where is he and what is he doing? He fired these questions back at the AIG. "Ursula, find Mattingly and report on his activities."

It took her a few minutes conferring with Condo and the geeks at the Deep Data Hex to suss out the Owl's location. It took a little more effort to determine what he was up to. Mattingly's time in the employ of General Turmoil had given him a good education in elusiveness and outright misdirection. He also developed a comprehensive knowledge of electronic warfare and cyber-attacks. If anyone could cripple **SOLARWIND**, it would be him. But there had to be some significant profit in it or why go to the major time and expense that would be required. Someone else was behind the threats but Ursula couldn't yet identify who the culprit is or what their motive could be. Frustrating!

"Doctor Bear, he's in Orlando, hiding in a thrill ride theme park, *Whirled World*. He has all his hacking equipment and malware set up in one of the park's server farms. We don't think he's quite ready to stage his assault on **SOLARWIND**. He's hired on at the park as one of the computer technicians that keep the amusements running. I don't think the park management has any idea who he really is. Do you want to blow the whistle on him?"

"Not yet! Someone's behind him. I want to know who that is. I do have one call I want to make. Ursula, get me Special Agent Honey Badger of the FBI."

*****

It took a while for the ship to shore connection but the Zoom call finally went through and The Badger appeared. The white stripe down the center of her grey head led past two piercing eyes to a twitching snout. A threatening stare, no doubt practiced in front of a mirror to cause no end of discomfort to her victims. She announced herself. "Special Agent Badger. Oh Hi, Octavius!" The frown disappeared and she actually smiled. "How are you? Where are you?'

"Fine, I'm on a cruise ship in the Caribbean."

"Lucky you! I'm in an office in Detroit. What's up!"

"I think we have a situation you folks may be interested in. What is the FBI's responsibilities as far as cruise ships go."

"I assume you're not interested in Great Lakes cruises which I might handle."

"No, let's try the tropics."

"Hold on a sec and let me check the regs. By the way. Thanks again for the assist with that drug lord in New Orleans."

"The ladies enjoyed it. Mlle Woof is off on a new career as a result. She and Sir Otto have developed a theatrical act with Tarot cards and a lot of slapstick. She calls herself Madame Giselle. They're performing in the theater and lounges on this ship."

"Sir Otto?"

"Yeah! He was knighted as Sir Otto the Magnificent by Emperor Merow of Orient on Exoplanet Orb for rescuing his kidnapped daughter."

"Well, give him my congratulations. Let's see! What's the name of the ship and what criminal activity are we looking into?"

"*SOLARWIND,* Solar Seas Cruise Lines, American owned and flagged. The possible crime is ransomware. The probable perp is Mattingly Owl. He's in Orlando. But I'm sure someone else is paying for his services. The attack may take place on the waters near St. Thomas or San Juan."

"Well those are American territories and American waters at least within twelve miles. Ransomware again? I still remember that yo-yo Caleb Cassowary. Have you paid off all the damage he caused?"

"Not yet, but we're getting there."

"Mattingly Owl. That name rings a bell. Oh, yeah. He worked for General Turmoil, didn't he?"

"Not anymore. He's gone freelance and not for the good. I think he's up to full time extortion and this ship is his target. Although he hasn't demanded money. At least, not yet."

"OK, while we've been jawing, I found the reg that applies to cruise ships. Let me translate from bureaucratese. Ahem!"

" *Quote: The authority of the FBI to investigate criminal offenses and enforce laws of the United States on cruise ships on the high seas or territorial waters of the United States depends on several factors: The location of the vessel, the nationality of the perpetrator or victim, the ownership of the vessel, the points of embarkation and debarkation, and the country in which the vessel is flagged all play a role in determining whether there is federal authority to enforce the laws of the United States. Unquote.*"

She went on. "From what you've told me, it all fits. We have a right to investigate this situation. Shall we drag this larcenous Owl in? I'll have to contact our Special Agent in San Juan, Fernando Hermano. He's a Hawk. A real one with feathers. I'll see if I can get myself involved. I could use a few days in Florida or the Caribbean Isles. What makes this cruise ship such a special target?"

"It's different." He proceeded to describe the vessel. When he finished, he said "I'll send you a picture and specs."

She whistled. "I can see where the government would want to take an interest in protecting that one. Be back to you shortly. I'll have to find my flip-flops if I'm heading South. Expect to hear from Fernando."

"Is this Fernando up on ransomware and cruise ship extortion?"

"Oh yes, that's one of the reasons he's assigned to the Caribbean. That, drugs, and money laundering."

"We had a messy money laundering exercise on our trip to Australia." *(See Book 16 – The Case Down Under)*

"I know. Bruce Wallaroo gave me chapter and verse. What's with you guys? Can't you lead a normal crime-free life?"

"Bruce claims I'll never retire. I'm beginning to think he's right."

"He usually is. Say hello to Belinda and the Twins, Maury and oh yes, Sir Otto and Madame Giselle. I'd love to catch their act."

"Maybe you'll get a chance to."

"OK, I'm going to hang up and call Fernando. I hope he's in San Juan. Where are you now."

"Nassau. We leave for St. Thomas this evening and then San Juan. Assuming we're still on a functioning ship."

"I'll call our office in Orlando and alert them to this Mattingly character. *Whirled World?* Theme parks, theme parks, theme parks! Thank God, there's no FBI Park. I'd probably end up as a walk around character. Cinderella Badger!"

"We'd need to find you an Agent Charming!"

They both laughed and cut off the Zoom session.

Chapter Sixteen

As the SOLARWIND goes sailing by,
The Great Bear gets his San Juan reply
He has quite a talk
With Fernando, a hawk
Who's a star at Carib FBI.

At the VIP pool, the Twins had just returned from the midday buffet. They were munching on shrimp fajitas and working away on their next extravaganza – *Bears at Sea*. Belinda had loaded up a plate for herself and was getting ready to return for a little sunbathing after her brief interview with Harriet Hare. She wondered what, if anything would come of that.

A smiling Freddi Fox, jaunty tan and white tail waving in the sea breeze, approached. "Bearoness, thank you so much for giving that interview to Harriet. She's been giving us a lot of good ink. Could you possibly set up a get together with that adorable Sir Otto and the lovely Madame Giselle? Harriet would eat it up. She's sooo superstitious!"

"I'm sure that could be arranged. Giselle could give her a private Tarot reading. Who knows about her future."

The Social Directress' smile faded. "Who knows about *our* future?"

"What do you mean?"

"All these meeting with the command staff and the bigshots from Fort Lauderdale. And your husband. Something is going on. I can't get much out of the Captain or the Purser. Diomede, the Security Officer looks like he lost his best friend. I've heard the Engineer refer to the **SOLARWIND** as a doom ship. When I ask, I keep getting told, 'Keep the passengers and reporters happy and occupied.' Well, of course. That's my job. But I could do it a lot better if I knew what's happening. Are we still getting threats?"

"Not that I know of. The Octavians are trying to get to the bottom of those messages. They think they have a few clues. We'll see."

"Who is this Madam Catt – Chita? No sooner did she show up on the ship and she got sent off with that hunky Jaguar and that cute Meerkat on a trip back to the States."

"She's doing some research for Octavius. By the way, she handles a lot of UUI's publicity and ad work. She's a real original. When she gets back, she'll need to meet Harriet. The columnist could learn a lot from her. So could you. She has a show business background. She's a singer and dancer. Maybe you could talk her into performing. And of course, there are my old buddies, Bearyl and Bearnice. Maury has them booked for several of your shows. You've got a tough job, Freddi. I wish I could make it easier for you."

"Thanks! I came by to pick up your Twins. It's almost time for our first Trivia contest. Mmm! Hey, kids, those fajitas smell good."

Arabella and McTavish had been performing a triple header – snarfing their buffet spoils, working on *Bears at Sea* and taking in the conversation between Bel and the Social Directress. Arabella nudged her sibling. "Doom ship! Make sure we get that in the game."

They finished their Mexican meal, grabbed the laptop with a passive Ursula on board and shouted. "OK, Ms. Fox, let's pursue some Trivia."

Bel shook her head. "Don't cheat."

Arabella put on her most innocent and winsome face while holding the AIG laden laptop. "Us cheat? Really, Mother. How could you think such a thing? Wait till the scavenger hunt tomorrow!"

Bursts of laughter! Off they went.

The Bearoness rose, put the towels in the bin and went to find Octavius. Something should be up by now and worth discussing.

*****

Octavius had just hung up on his call with Special Agent Badger when Belinda came though the door of the suite. "Hello! Who were you talking to?

"Special Agent Badger. I'm calling in the FBI on this one. There's a Special Agent in San Juan I'm expecting to hear from. Fernando Hermano. The Solar Seas Company may not like it but they'll like a ransomware strike even less."

"I have our Advanced Super Computing Center back at the Hexagon on high alert. I think some of those super-techies are salivating at the idea of getting into a cyberwar. I trust Condo and Byzz to keep them in check."

"Do you really believe Mattingly will attack?"

"I hope he doesn't but I have to assume he will and act accordingly. How was your swim?"

"OK! The pool is a bit warm. I understand we'll have an opportunity to swim in the ocean later in the trip. I'm looking forward to that. Of course, there are always the island beaches. What's St. Thomas like?"

"It's a combination. Charlotte Amalie has both natural beauty and a thriving city life. You have choices. Elegant dining, nightlife, duty-free shopping *(are you listening, Chita?)* and even submarine rides. But you can also relax on St. Thomas' many beaches, trek or go diving especially at Coral World Ocean Park. Not exactly the Great Barrier Reef in Australia that you so loved but fun nonetheless."

"Good. I'm sure the Twins will be up for it. I hope you settle this cyber mess quickly so we can all relax on the rest of the trip. We only want excitement of the fun variety. No more violence."

The Great Bear's cell phone rang. Puerto Rico number. Octavius signaled Ursula to join in the connection. "This is Octavius Bear."

"Hello, Doctor Bear! This is Special Agent Fernando Hermano of the San Juan office of the FBI. I understand from Special Agent Badger that you may have a situation we should be interested in."

"Yes, Agent Hermano. A ransomware attack on a cruise ship. I understand that may be in your line of work."

"Yes indeed. Fill me in!"

Chapter Seventeen

Our brave trio is back from their trip.
In St. Thomas awaiting the ship.
On the trail of some clues,
They must relay the news.
They disgustedly came up with zip.

The tower at St. Thomas International Airport cleared the Embraer Legacy 600 for an approach and the Octavian threesome plus Ursula belted themselves in anticipating landing not far from Charlotte Amalie and an evening's rest *(or otherwise?)* The **SOLARWIND** would be tying up at close-by Havensight Dock next morning. Assuming nothing untoward happened to it between Nassau and St. Thomas.

All the way from New Orleans, Chita, Jack and Ursula reviewed and re-reviewed the situation. The consensus was Mardi Gras Cruise Lines were not involved in the threats in spite of what Agrippa said.

They sent that opinion on to Octavius and he relayed it to the rest of the shipboard group, including Captain Lion and his staff. The Solar Seas management, especially the COO and CFO, were less willing to exculpate their rival cruise line. However, Wally Wapiti, the lawyer, marketeer and security officer won over and they all finally reluctantly agreed.

Octavius had announced that they knew where Mattingly was but were unwilling to move on him until they could determine who else was involved. He also assured them that the Owl's attack would be forestalled by the Advanced Computing Center. the minute he launched it."

As usual, Loretta Lynx protested. "We have to take your word that your geeks can defeat this Owl. I'm not the least bit confident. I still think you and your so-called Octavians are behind all this. I think you want to ruin Solar Seas. You want the **SOLARWIND** for yourself. You want to add a cruise line to your UUI empire."

She got the Solar Seas management's attention with that last remark. Could she be on to something?

Octavius didn't even bother to respond to this nonsense. Maybe the Twins wanted their own cruise ship but he didn't. Bel was talking about adding a pier at Polar Paradise for Arctic cruisers. Fine! More business for the resort. But somebody else's ships. Not his!

*****

Notes from Tour Guide Maury:

Chita and Jack decided that before meeting the ship tomorrow, they were going to have a night on the town in Charlotte Amalie. After all, back in the 1600's the town had a Danish name that translated into "beer hall." In 1691 the Town got a more respectable title - Charlotte Amalie in honor of Danish King Christian V's wife, Charlotte Amalie of Hesse-Kassel.

In 1917, the U.S. purchased St. Thomas, St. John and St. Croix from Denmark for 25 million dollars, creating the US Virgin Islands. Between 1921 and 1936, the city was called St. Thomas by the United States. In 1936 the capital was recognized as Charlotte Amalie.

The economy depends on tourism, handicrafts, jewelry, and the production of rum, bay rum, and jams. As well as being the political capital, it is the port capital of the U.S. Virgin Islands. Charlotte Amalie is the third most popular cruise ship destination in the Caribbean behind Nassau and Cozumel. Up to eleven cruise ships can occupy the harbor on any given day. About 1.5 plus million tourists visit on average per year.

Attractions include Blackbeard's Castle which is one of the most visited in the Town. That appealed to Chita's larcenous but reformed soul as well as the prospect of some island rum. Off they went, taking me with them. Ursula kept contact with Octavius.

*****

Back on board the **SOLARWIND,** another hectic evening of fun, food and froth was proceeding apace as the ship made its way toward St. Thomas. The Bears and Octavians were once again seated in the Gourmet Gardens. Across the room Glady Vaquero who had succeeded in landing a table in the posh restaurant, was loudly annoying all in sight berating a server for some infraction, real or imagined.

The well-dressed Twins looked over from their non-alcoholic punch drinks. McTavish winked at Frau Ilse and the Colonel. "You guys were in the military. Can't you command her to shut up? Gee, you should have heard them earlier. They accused their opponents of cheating at shuffleboard. She was so drunk she couldn't keep the disks on the court. Her husband was as bad as she was. They're definitely material for *Bears at Sea.* They're probably material for being thrown overboard or walking the plank." They all laughed.

Freddi Fox came over to the tables. A pair of well but conservatively dressed sheep accompanied her. "Good evening, Octavians. I hope you're enjoying yourselves in this delightful restaurant. I just wanted to take a moment to introduce the Shearings to those of you who haven't met them. Sylvia and Gideon Shearing, meet Doctor Octavius Bear and his charming mate, Bearoness Belinda Béarnaise Bruin Bear *(nee Black)*. These are their children McTavish and Arabella and these are their Associates, the Octavians." In a marvelous demonstration of memory, she rattled off the names of the entire team sitting there.

Octavius stood up to his full nine feet and said, "Delighted to meet you. I understand that you two are the most faithful of the Old Faithful VIPs. You must spend more time on the water than on the land. Are you from Texas?"

Gideon, the ram, bleated gently and said, "Yes, sir. We are, but as you say, we spend most of our days on cruise ships, especially those of Solar Seas. We are in finance out of Austin. Texas Capital. That's actually our company name. Confuses people. Oddly enough, the Vaqueros over there are our clients. He's a billionaire oilman. A little too forceful for our taste but a very good source of revenue. Sylvia and I, like you, are partially retired. Where are my manners? Sylvia, say hello."

The ewe, who had been standing modestly by during this dialogue, baaed softly and smiled. "I'm so pleased to meet you. Ms. Fox has been telling us about you all. You must lead such exciting lives."

Otto chuckled, "Too exciting."

Sylvia giggled. "I saw your act in the theater. It was brilliant."

Giselle smiled. "Merci, Madame. Perhaps you will let me do a reading for you."

Gideon interrupted, I'm afraid we don't subscribe to fortune telling."

Sylvia shrugged, "Oh Gideon. It's just for fun. Yes, Madame. I'd like that."

Gideon frowned and said, "I think it's time we all set about having our dinners. Very pleased to meet you all. No doubt we will see each other as the cruise progresses." He turned to Freddi who led them across the room near where the Vaqueros were seated."

The oilman bellowed. "Hey, Gideon. I hope you're making money for me while you're on this ridiculous ship. Let's see those investments grow …or else. Waiter, don't just stand there. More champagne."

The sheep pretended not to hear but all the other dinners did. Disgusted looks and shaking heads.

Arabella nudged McTavish. "Maybe we don't want them in our game, after all. We have enough jerks already. Everyone! Did you know we won both Trivial Pursuit contests today?"

Applause!

Belinda mumbled. "You and Ursula."

McTavish smiled. "We're entering the Multi-Deck Scavenger Hunt tomorrow night after dinner. Who knows what we'll find?"

Chapter Eighteen

With the FBI now on the case
It's becoming a high powered race.
In Orlando, the Owl
Plots transgressions most foul.

We are off on a ransomware chase.

Convinced by Octavius that the FBI should be involved, Special Agent Fernando Hermano boarded a small prop puddle jumper and covered the 68 air miles from San Juan to St. Thomas in about 45 minutes. He had agreed to have Agent Honey Badger join him in running down this ransomware case.

It took a little persuasion and use of vacation time for her to get her Midwest superiors to agree to her heading to the Caribbean and a cruise ship. It took no effort at all for Octavius to get the *SOLARWIND* Purser to set aside a couple of cabins for them since her job may well depend on how this caper comes off. Agent Badger would be landing at STT at just about the time the cruise ship would be reaching Havensight Dock. The two agents had agreed to meet and then reach out to Octavius Bear.

Chita, Jaguar Jack and I would also be reboarding the ship at roughly the same time. Conferences and consultations galore. The eight onboard Ursulas were going to be busy, recording, researching, recommending and, as necessary repelling the attacks.

Little did the thousand plus tourists know what was going on to keep them safe and preserve their vacation investments.

As the ship neared Charlotte Amalie, Captain Lion called Octavius for a one on one get together.

"What do you think, Doctor Bear? If the Mystic Mardi Gras Company isn't behind this, who is? I'm not interested in commanding a floating hulk and answering a flood of questions and accusations."

The Bear paused. "Questions and accusations! I wonder! I'll be back."

The *SOLARWIND* eased into the Charlotte Amalie harbor on its way to its berth at Havensight Docks. Its peculiar configuration of wind and solar sails and low aerodynamic profile attracted significant attention just as it had in Nassau and back in Ft. Lauderdale. No doubt, it would continue to bring out sightseers, photographers and the press as it continued on its Caribbean journey. Hopefully, the publicity would not include images of a crippled vessel being towed toward drydock after debarking all of its passengers.

Once again, the passengers were lined up for their port day departures. The cabs lined up on the pier waiting to take the adventurers on the short ride to downtown Charlotte Amalie.

Special Agent Hermano got out of an incoming taxi and the hawk was about to spread his wings and fly up the gangway when he spied a badger wrestling with baggage as she got out of another cab. He hopped over and said, "Can I give you a claw, Ms.?"

The badger didn't look up but grunted. "No thanks. I could use a porter."

"I'll see what I can do."

She recognized the voice, turned around and laughed. "Oh, Fernando. It's you. There's a red cap. Flash your badge at him! Mine's in my luggage."

"Tsk, tsk! An FBI agent should always be ready to identify him or herself."

"I yell a lot."

The porter came over with his dolly, stacked her bags and Fernando's back pack and headed up the gangway to the security desk.

"Honey, you look like you're planning to make a trip out of this. Why so much luggage?"

"I am making a trip out of this. I'm using my accumulated vacation. Octavius Bear has us booked in the VIP zone and I intend to get full use out of it. It helps to know a gazillionaire. And no, there's no conflict of interest. Wait a second. There's someone I know."

Chita, Jack and I had gotten out of another cab, spotted the FBI agent and waved. She waved back and skittered over.

"Hi! Let me introduce you to Fernando Hermano, Special Agent in our San Juan office. *(Paw and claw shakes)*

110

Fernando screeched lightly. "It looks like there are as many creatures boarding this ship as getting off. I assume we're all working on the same issue."

"Keeping this ship on an even keel? Right! We're getting together with Octavius ASAP in his Imperial Suite on the Empire deck."

They checked in with Ship Security and were met by Freddi. "Hello Maury, Senor Jack and Madame Catt. Welcome back. How was New Orleans?"

I replied. "Unproductive, Freddi. Let me introduce two members of the Federal Bureau of Investigation. Special Agents Honey Badger and Fernando Hermano."

The Social Directress' eyes opened wide. "The FBI. So we do have a serious problem on our paws!"

"We don't know for sure but we're not taking any chances. Can you or one of the stewards show these two agents to their cabins and then to Doctor Bear's suite? Please don't identify them as law officers. We're keeping this situation as confidential as we can"

"Oh. of course!" She called over one of the attendants and gave him instructions.

They reached two balcony cabins at the stern of the Empire Deck. *Unfortunately,* next to the Vaqueros. *Fortunately,* they had gone to Charlotte Amalie, no doubt in search of some native rum.

Chapter Nineteen

With the Big Easy Three's failed report
We return to Agrippa's retort.
He claims he's not a fault

For a malware assault.
If not, who hatched the plot to extort?

Carlos responded to the knock on the doors and Octavius rose from the sofa he was sharing with Belinda. The Twins and most of the other Octavians had gone on a tour of Charlotte Amalie. Madame Giselle wanted a little more glitzy jewelry for her act and the city's duty free shoppes were cheaper than the shipboard vendors.

"Come in, come in. Good to see you again, Agent Badger. I hope you've negotiated a little R&R along with this assignment. Nice to meet you, Agent Hermano."

"Please, Doctor Bear, call me Fernando."

"Fine and I'm Octavius. Ah. here come the Big Easy Three. Carlos, can you scare up some coffee and snacks?" He turned to me. "Maury, you, Chita and Jack are convinced Mystical Mardi Gras is not behind Mattingly Owl and Ursula agrees?"

" 'Fraid so!"

"Well, who the hell is and what do they want? Maury! Call Dudley Diomede, the Security Officer and see if he can bring Agrippa up here. I want to squeeze my lying step-brother till it hurts. Thanks!"

Honey Badger frowned. "While we're waiting, bring Fernando and me up to speed on what this nefarious Owl can do. We've been involved in ransomware before. I'm still smarting from that Crazy Cassowary's antics. It was clear what he wanted. Complete power and money. This seems different."

It is. Or at least I think it is. The Owl is working for someone and Agrippa is involved but not in charge. That doesn't surprise me. He couldn't pull this off. I'm glad you're here, Fernando. I think this is going to go down between St. Thomas and Puerto Rico. We're going to need your authority."

"As for what he can do. Total chaos. All of the ship's systems down. No power! No control! No services essential or otherwise. Dead in the water. I'm reasonably certain my folks at the Hexagon can keep it from happening or recover from it quickly if it does. Does the FBI have agents on standby in Orlando? That's where the Owl is hidden away in a thrill ride theme park. *Whirled World*! Great name."

Fernando screeched. "If he starts up, we'll come down on him like the proverbial ton of bricks. I have a direct high speed link to our Orlando office. They can be there in minutes after we discover he's trying to cripple this ship. Your folks may have to do a little clean up on board but we should be able to minimize the impact. Why do you think he'll act between here and Puerto Rico?"

"Because the media leaves the **SOLARWIND** in San Juan. So does Solar Seas top management. The plotters want maximum public damage and embarrassment to happen before that. The brass need to be caught up in an inextricable mess. Worldwide scandal! Possible bankruptcy. I lived through something like it. It's no fun. Ah, here comes the coffee and my step-brother."

The Security Officer entered with Agrippa in tow. He was wearing pawcuffs. "I say, Octavius these cuffs are a bit much."

Dudley Diomede replied. "As long as he can escape from the ship onto dry land, the cuffs stay on."

'Octavius smiled. "Out of my paws, 'Grippa. Let me introduce two members of the FBI. Special Agents Badger and Hermano. They think piracy and extortion are at work here and you're involved."

"I'm not a pirate and I didn't have anything to do with those threats."

The Badger said, "Ahh! But you know about the threats. You wrote them."

"I did no such thing."

"Look, step-brother mine, make it easier on yourself. Right now, you're up for Fraud - using fake credentials to gain employment as manager of this ship's casino! That will earn you some jail time. Don't make it worse by aiding and abetting piracy, willful damage to this vessel and injuring its passengers and crew."

"You can't hang that one on me."

Fernando stared at him, "Oh, yes we can if this Mattingly Owl cyberattacks the ship. You're involved all right. Now, what's his plan and who's paying him?"

"Not me. I'm just the go-between. Oh, All right. He's going to launch his computer assault right after we leave St. Thomas and everybody is back on the ship. Except me. I was supposed to get off in Charlotte Amalie but this Albatross Security Officer has other ideas. *SOLARWIND* is not supposed to reach San Juan except under tow."

"What about the press and the Solar Seas management?"

"There's a rescue boat arranged to take them on to San Juan so they can write and broadcast their stories. Members of the company management and some selected VIPs will be in the party. The President and Lawyer will be doing publicity and legal damage control. No doubt there will be press conferences galore. "

Chita laughed. "So much for staying with the sinking ship. I assume the Captain and his crew will still be on board fighting to keep *SOLARWIND* afloat and viable."

"Of course, they have to keep the passengers safe and avoid panicking."

Jack scrunched up his formidable face, "I don't get it. Is management involved in this plot? And if so, why?"

"Not all of them!"

Octavius slapped a paw on the table. "Let me guess. This is the brainchild of Loretta Lynx, the CFO. She's been opposing any protective measures all along and poo-pooing the threats."

Agrippa nodded, "She wrote the threats. She and Coleman Cougar, the COO. They want the Board of Directors to fire Wally Wapiti as a result of this disaster and put Coleman in his place. Loretta will become COO."

Octavius shook his head. "The fools. All this to topple the CEO. Those two will be arrested and the rest of the Corporate Office fired except for the lawyer, Emilia Emu. She'll have her wings full. Solar Seas may not even survive."

Honey Badger growled, "I've heard enough. Fernando, let's order up the Orlando office and take down this Owl. Commander Diomede, place Loretta Lynx and Coleman Cougar under arrest!"

The Great Bear interrupted. "Hold on, everyone. None of this has happened yet. All we have is my step-brother's say so and it's well known what a terrible phony he is. A bear faced liar who forged references and recommendations to land a casino manager's job. We have to let this farce play out."

"Ursula, you and your companions will go on critical standby to fend off the Owl's cyberattack as soon as the ship leaves port. Agrippa, who is supposed to signal Mattingly to begin his ransomware activities?"

"Not me. I assume it will be the Lynx."

"Ursula, I want one of you to monitor all communication traffic to and from Loretta Lynx and Coleman Cougar. They'll probably use an encrypted code to get our friend in *Whirled World* active."

"Meanwhile, let's gather the Captain and the Deck officers and fill them in. What do you think, Bel? Should we involve the Purser and her Staff?"

"Of course, they have all those passengers to worry about."

"Right! What was I thinking? Commander Diomede, can you get all the officers up at the Bridge Conference room?"

*****

It took a little doing since the **SOLARWIND** was heavily engaged in turnaround activities disembarking over a thousand passengers at Havensight and preparing for the evening's transfer to San Juan.

After about an hour, Octavius, Chita, Jack and I along with Belinda and the two FBI agents were shown into the bridge conference room. Commander Diomede had Agrippa, still in cuffs under control.

The Captain and both the Deck and Hotel officers were gathered there. They were clearly anxious to get back to their assignments. "Doctor Bear, can we make this quick? This is a busy day for us. I don't think I've met these two folks and why is our former casino manager here."

Octavius introduced the FBI agents and said, "My stepbrother who you know as Albeart has a story to tell."

With prodding and much shuffling, Agrippa told his sorry tail.

The Captain, Purser and engineer were livid. "You're telling us members of the Corporate office are planning to sabotage their own ship and endanger our passengers and all our crew?"

Fernando screeched, "That's what he's saying."

"Commander Diomede, arrest the CFO and COO immediately. Can you stop this Owl in Orlando?"

"Wait, Captain! We don't have sufficient evidence to arrest them or knock off the Owl's activity. Our friends from the FBI are ready to step in immediately here and back in Florida but we have to let the culprits initiate the attack to have enough proof against them. Albeart's or as I know him, Agrippa's testimony can be torn apart by any near competent lawyer. I know it's dangerous but I have my anti-ransomware team on high alert and they are extremely competent. Can you and your teams go about your business and act as if everything is normal?"

The Chief Engineer cursed. "I'll have to inform my technicians, sir. They need to know how to react." The Chief Purser dittoed.

The Captain nodded. "Of course, your teams' behavior will be key. Doctor Bear, Tell us about this anti-ransomware team of yours"

Reluctantly, Octavius revealed the identities of the Ursulas and described the UUI Advanced Super Computing Center at the Hexagon. He explained decryption speeds and quantum computing techniques that will search out and defeat any malware holding systems, networks and data for ransom. He alluded to UUI's experience with Caleb Cassowary and his vanquished extra-planetary warfare. The Octavians and Agent Badger supported his claims but he wasn't sure anyone of the ships officers, except perhaps the Chief Engineer believed him.

"OK," said Captain Lion, "We'll play by your rules but I'm not going to allow my ship to be overcome by a couple of overly ambitious company nuts and their techie raider."

Octavius nodded. "Trust us, Captain. It won't come to that."

*****

The day progressed and the ship was readied to receive its vacationers back and proceed to the Port of San Juan. The sea distance of 68 nautical miles was a short one but this time it was filled with anticipation on the bridge, engine rooms and the Imperial Suite. Two Ursulas were monitoring Loretta Lynx and Coleman Cougar. Agrippa was back in his cell, still pawcuffed and complaining bitterly. Orlando FBI was on alert. Captain Lion and Staff Captain Montmorency Mongoose checked in with Octavius periodically. No issues in the engine room or the server farms.

Dinner was informal and served in random restaurants, cafeterias and suites via room service. Chita, Jack, Agents Badger and Hermano joined Octavius, Belinda, the Twins and me for another splendid meal. No planned entertainments were on offer. The bars were filled. Impromptu karaoke sessions rang through the corridors. The vacationers, worn out from a day of touring Charlotte Amalie, were lazily thinking through their two-day stop in the capital of Puerto Rico.

The Development of Civilization Volume18
Part 6
Quantum Computing

From "An Introduction to Faunapology"

by Octavius Bear Ph.D.

In previous volumes of these casebooks we have discussed various phenomena and characteristics of the quantum universe. "Strange" doesn't begin to describe it. We are dealing with quantum mechanics, the scientific principles addressing the infinitesimal.

Not too long ago, we believed the atom was the smallest physical element. No longer. Now we can comfortably talk about the sub-atomic realm - electrons, positrons photons, leptons, muons, taus. OK, maybe not so comfortably.

Somewhere between the very, very small and the unimaginably large, there is a major disconnect among the theorists. Quantum mechanics and Newtonian physics don't match up! There have been many attempts to patch over the gaps. In the process, the theoretical multiverse has acquired as many as eleven dimensions including space - time.

There is one principle of quantum theory that should interest us at this point in our narrative. Quantum superposition at the sub-atomic level. Don't despair. We'll explain!

In 1935, a cat named Schrodinger showed how superposition would operate in the everyday world. As long as we do not observe or measure it, a subatomic object can exist in any number (a superposition) of states. It is only when we turn our attention to the object that the superposition is lost, and the object appears in only one of its potential states. Trust me! It's true!

One of these objects is the fundamental component of QC (Quantum Computing)- the Qubit.

We are all familiar with the Bit – the basic element of all of our conventional computing devices. A Bit is the fundamental stuff on which computer design is based – the binary 1's <u>or</u> 0's found in electronic *storage and processing devices such as the transistor. All electronic digital data is nothing more or less than a string of bits. (Bytes are multiple bits packaged together.)Programs are specialized bit strings designed to provide instructions to digital devices - computers, phones and other communication devices, robots, watches, sensors, special purpose industrial, medical, entertainment machines and the like. We are immersed in bits and bytes.*

But along comes the Qubit. It has one exceedingly important difference from its predecessor. <u>It can represent a 1 and a 0 at the same time!</u> Quantum mechanics, somewhat miraculously, enables the qubit to be in a "superposition" of both states simultaneously, a property which is fundamental to quantum mechanics and quantum computing.

In conventional systems, a bit would have to be in one state or the other. Not so with the Qubit. It can be in both.

So what? It sounds like a physicist's, mathematician's or computer geek's toy.

It's much more than that! There are classes of problems and processes so extensive and involved that today's bit-based, classic computers have no hope of dealing with them successfully. Some have been estimated to take thousands of years using conventional hardware and software. The term Quantum Supremacy was coined to describe situations where, by dealing with all potential paths at once, Qubit driven hardware and software would support possible applications that would forever be beyond the legacy system's ability.

Here's a short list of environments where some of these possible applications exist. Clearly, not every problem in these arenas requires Qubit design. Bit based systems are already making great contributions.

- *Cybersecurity*
- *Artificial Intelligence*
- *Computer Animation and Simulation*
- *Drug Development and Genetic Research*
- *Weather Forecasting and Climate Change*
- *Financial Modeling*
- *Energy Forms including Batteries*

- *Traffic Optimization*
- *Differential and Integral Calculus Computations*

We must quickly add that most of these QC apps are in their infancy. OK, what makes Quantum Computing so swift and capable when it can be applied. (Which is not always the case.) <u>In a nutshell, rather than having to perform tasks sequentially, like most traditional computers, quantum computers can run vast numbers of parallel computations at very high speed.</u> Not all applications fit, so quantum computing is not the answer to every IT manager's prayer. Don't ditch your current systems, some of which are already designed to run parallel processes but not at the speed, complexity and scope of QC.

Another fly in the technological ointment is the fact that today's Quantum devices are notoriously unstable. Error rates are quite high. The device must <u>maintain</u> dual state superpositioning -1 <u>and</u> 0. Otherwise it will fall back to a single state – 1 <u>or</u> 0 and behave like a conventional bit driven system. Today's quantum prototypes are very sensitive to physical interference and errors are frequent. Error correction algorithms and design changes are being developed.

There are many opinions about the future of QC. Sceptics abound but the enthusiasts are also numerous. Once stable and commercially viable devices are possible, if ever, what are the research, military, education and military markets? Can QC devices be effectively embodied in aircraft, vehicles, ships, weather stations and the like that can make use of the high speed, superpositioning phenomena or will they remain semi-experimental oddities?

Finally, what does all this have to do with encryption and decryption – Ursula 16's specialty? Cryptosystems hide an immense number of private and secret communication programs, files and protocols, from email, financial and defense data to internet retail transactions. <u>They are also the basis of ransomware. Hostile encryption!</u> Current encryption relies on the fact that no one yet has the computing power to find the correct encryption key but a mature quantum computer could try every option and find it very shortly. That's what Ursula is doing in our story with a little help from her friends at the Advanced Super Computing Center.

Chapter Twenty

The conspirators finally are caught.
They're the ones whom Octavius thought.
They cooked up an attack.
Now they'll have to look back
And regret all the trouble they wrought.

At precisely 8 PM, the ship's horn sounded and the dock crew released the hawsers allowing **SOLARWIND** to slowly move away from the dock, out through the channel and into the ocean.

"Battle stations! 30 miles out in open water, a coded signal flew on its way from **SOLARWIND** to *Whirled World* in Orlando. The Ursula monitoring the Lynx swiftly decrypted the message. "Execute King's Ransom!" They had her. As backup, Coleman Cougar sent a matching signal. The chump! The two FBI agents raced to the conspirators' suites. Amid screams and shouts, they arrested the two executives and dumped them in the brig next door to Agrippa.

The computers on the ship's Deck One briefly fluttered. Up in Kentucky, at the UUI Deep Data Hexagon, an array of quantum speed devices swung into action, canceling the instructions coming from Mattingly Owl's network and decrypting any passwords or malware he had implanted. Up on the ship's Bridge and down on Deck Zero, there were sighs of relief.

Agents from FBI Orlando descended on the thrill ride theme park and dragged Mattingly Owl out of his hidden nest. He tried unsuccessfully to destroy the evidence before being carted off to an Orlando jail.

The Captain, security officer and purser were brought up to speed by the FBI. Shock mixed with disgust. The Greyhound said it best. "Reckless and total disregard for the safety of this ship, its crew and passengers in order to advance their personal ambitions. I hope they rot."

SOLARWIND continued on her short journey past the Castillo San Felipe del Morro to Port San Juan. The passengers and most of the crew were uninformed of the brief drama that had just unfolded. Some passengers were betting away at the casino (without its manager) for the short time it would be open. The unaware press were polishing up their final reports. They had been submitting copy and video all during the cruise. This would be the finale. Harriet Hare was staying on doing more interviews as the ship sailed around the Caribbean.

Captain Lion called Wally Wapiti and the Solar Sea executives up to the Bridge Conference Room. Octavius, Belinda, Chita, Jack and I were there along with the FBI agents. The Purser, Security Officer and Engineer were already seated together.

The CEO asked, "Is there new news? We're getting ready to leave the ship. Thanks, Captain and Purser Greyhound. Wait, we can't start this session yet. Where are Loretta and Coleman?"

The ship's Chief Security officer squawked, chittered and spread his massive wings. "They're in the brig waiting to be transferred to a San Juan jail along with Doctor Bear's stepbrother. Then on to Tampa for arraignment."

"Whaaaat?"

Octavius rumbled and told them the story. "They're going to be indicted on piracy, conspiracy and ransomware charges and attempts to overthrow the Solar Seas executive structure, especially you."

Emilia Emu, the Corporate Lawyer asked. "Do you have enough evidence to make it stick?"

"Plenty, all scientifically recorded."

"No wonder Loretta didn't want you to investigate. She and Coleman are toast."

Wapiti turned to the Corporate Security Officer and Lawyer. "Pablo and Emilia. I want you two to stay here in San Juan and make sure they don't escape or wiggle out of this. Come back with them to Lauderdale. We'll all go to Tampa. I want to watch their trials."

Epilogue

The Octavians zoomed to and fro.
Now their throttle is turning to 'slow'.
Is this really the time
For another grim crime?
Will this team ever get to let go?

Evening Two aboard the **SOLARWIND** in San Juan. The press had disappeared along with the Solar Seas Executives. The culprits had been taken into custody by the FBI and were being flown back under guard to the FBI Tampa Field Office to join their co-conspirator - Mattingly Owl who had been brought over from Orlando.

Fernando returned to his San Juan office but was on call to fly up to Tampa. Agent Honey Badger was staying on the ship spending her vacation time.

As a thank you from the Captain, Freddi Fox had organized a Ladies' Day tour of Old San Juan for the Octavian females. Belinda, Arabella, Chita, Frau Ilse, Madame Giselle, Agent Badger, Bearyl and Bearnice Blanc and Galatea Tigris. Harriet Hare came along. Touring, dining, champagne and shopping, shopping, shopping. Jewelry, mantillas, scarves, belts and sashes. All in a day's work.

Ernie Ermine got together a sport fishing expedition for the males. Octavius, McTavish, Sir Otto, Jaguar Jack, Lord David, Dancing Dan, Howard, the Colonel, Benedict Tigris and little ole' me. Nobody got seasick. Nobody caught anything. Everybody had drinks.

They came back to the ship and were getting ready for the journey to the next port of call. Grand Turk Island. Several days at sea to cover the over 390 nautical miles from San Juan would keep the **SOLARWIND's** staff super busy. Otto, Madame Giselle, Bearyl and Bearnice will all be doing their acts in the main theater. Belinda even consented to give a diving exhibition in the Lido pool. Harriet continues her interviews. Freddi and Ernie will be organizing games, events, challenges. Spa, gym and beauty appointments are getting tight. Once on the open sea, the casino expected to do land office business, sans Agrippa. One of the assistant managers had taken charge.

Promptly at 5 PM, the ship pulled away from the slip and headed out to open water. Tonight is the Multi Deck Scavenger Hunt, long awaited by the Twins *(and Ursula.)* Only the bridge, kitchens, sick bay, brig and engine decks are off limits. Most of the shoppes were closed.

Freddi Fox had organized a number of searcher teams with six members each. The Twins found themselves matched up with two middle-aged VIP wolverines and a teen-aged pair of male racoons. They had to find a bell, a picture of a blue whale, an old map of Havana, Cuba and a set of towel animals created each day by the cleaning staffs.

Like most of the teams, they decided to break up in search of the individual items. They drew straws. Arabella and McTavish got the towel animals. They decided this late in the evening all the towels on the Lido deck would have been used. They went to the VIP pool where nobody was around. But they found a couple of terry cloth giraffes. They were about to return to the starting point when Arabella noticed a large figure floating face down in the otherwise unoccupied pool. "Who is that? Tavi, Help! Get a security guard!"

McTavish stared for a moment and ran off to get help. Two guards rushed to the pool and jumped in to retrieve the floating body. They dragged him out and applied artificial respiration. Too late!

The Twins ran off to the Imperial Suite and rushed through the door knocking Carlos over in the process. "Mom, Dad! Guess what! A body! He's dead! We found him!"

Belinda reacted first. "Who's dead? What happened?"

Arabella caught her breath and sputtered. "We were looking for towel animals for the Scavenger Hunt and we saw him floating in the VIP pool. We called security. They're there now."

Before Bel could ask 'who' again, there was a knock on the door. Chief Security Officer Dudley Diomede entered. "Doctor Bear, Bearoness. Sorry to disturb you but we have an incident and I could use your help. We have a dead body at the VIP pool. Your kids discovered it."

McTavish looked shocked. "Are we in trouble? We didn't do anything except call security."

The Albatross shook his head and squawked, "No! No! You're fine." He looked at the Great Bear and Belinda. "It's that obnoxious Texas oil tycoon, Humphrey Vaquero. The guards thought he was drunk as usual and had fallen in. But then one of them noticed a stab wound in his back. This wasn't an accident. He was murdered."

Octavius got to his feet, looked at the bird and said, "Show me!'

As they left, Belinda shook her head. "Tavi, Tavi, Tavi! Oh, dear! Here we go again. Crime seems to follow us around. Are we ever going to be able to just relax and act like retired animals? We're on this ship for another seven days. How many more incidents will we have to deal with?"

THE END

THE BEAR FACED LIAR

BOOK 18

THE CASEBOOKS OF OCTAVIUS BEAR

About the Author

Harry DeMaio is a *nom de plume* of Harry B. DeMaio, successful author of several books on Information Security and Business Networks as well as the eighteen-volume *Casebooks of Octavius Bear.* He is also a published author for Belanger Books and the MX Sherlock Holmes series. A retired business executive, former consultant, information security specialist, elected official, private pilot, disk jockey and graduate school adjunct professor, he whiles away his time traveling and writing preposterous books, articles and stories.

He has appeared on many radio and TV shows and is an accomplished, frequent public speaker.

Former New York City natives, he and his extremely patient and helpful wife, Virginia, live in Cincinnati (and several other parallel universes.) They have two sons, Mark, living in Scottsdale, Arizona and Andrew. in Cortlandt Manor, New York, both of whom are quite successful and quite normal, thus putting the lie to the theory that insanity is hereditary.

His e-mail is hdemaio@zoomtown.com

You can also find him on Facebook.

His website is www.octaviusbearslair.com

His books are available on Amazon, Barnes and Noble, and other fine bookstores as well as directly from MX Publishing and Belanger Books.

www.ingramcontent.com/pod-product-compliance
Lightning Source LLC
Chambersburg PA
CBHW080543180626
46818CB00008B/3116